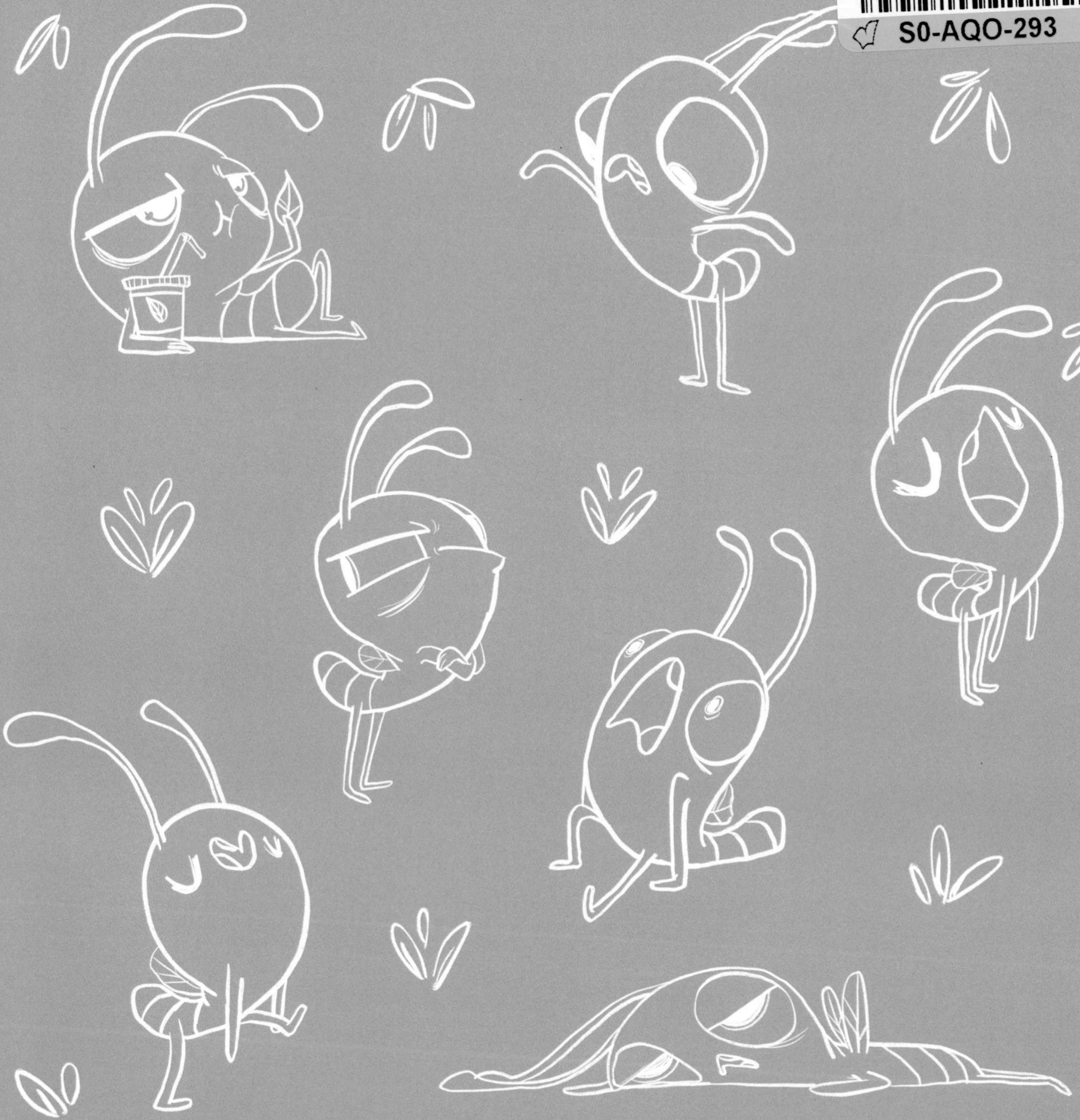

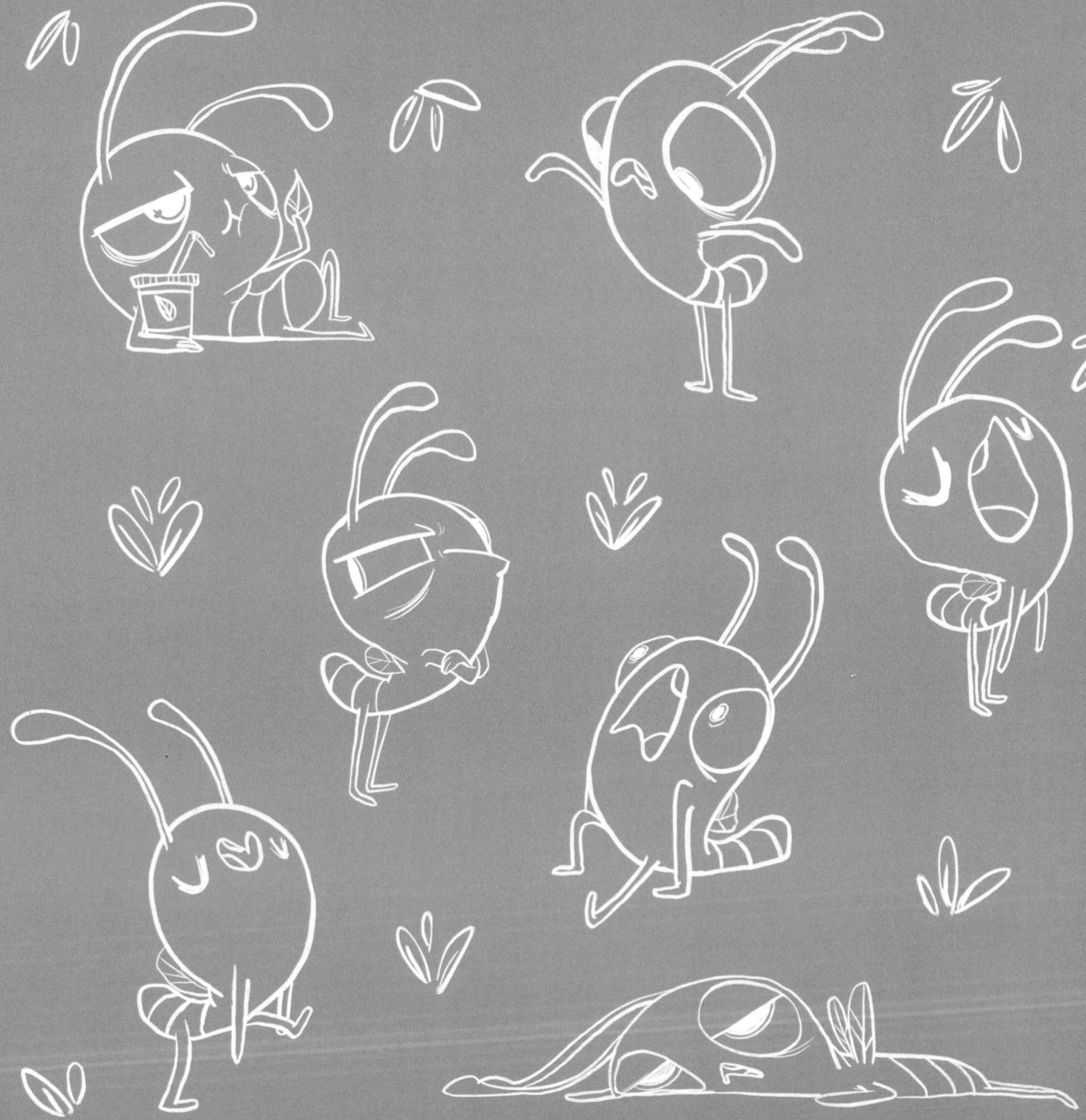

IT'S NOT EASY BEING A LAZY BUG

This book belongs to:

Adelina Weaver-Barnes

Dedicated to all the Lazy Bugs in my family,
Nishka, Rohan, Bhaumik, Navya, Ishaan, Saumya and Kuhu.
-P.T.

Dedicated to my loving parents,
Shirley and Alden Maclean.
-R.M.

Dedicated to my loving brothers and parents.
-M.F.

Library of Congress Control Number: 2020934216

Copyright@ 2020 by PenMagic Books LLC

Text and illustration copyright @2020 PenMagic Books LLC

First edition

ISBN 978-1-952821-05-9 (Paperback)

https://www.PenMagicBooks.com

PenMagic Books LLC provides special discounts when
purchased in larger volumes for premiums and promotional
purposes, as well as for fundraising and educational use.
Custom editions can also be created for special purposes.
In addition, supplemental teaching material can be
provided upon request.

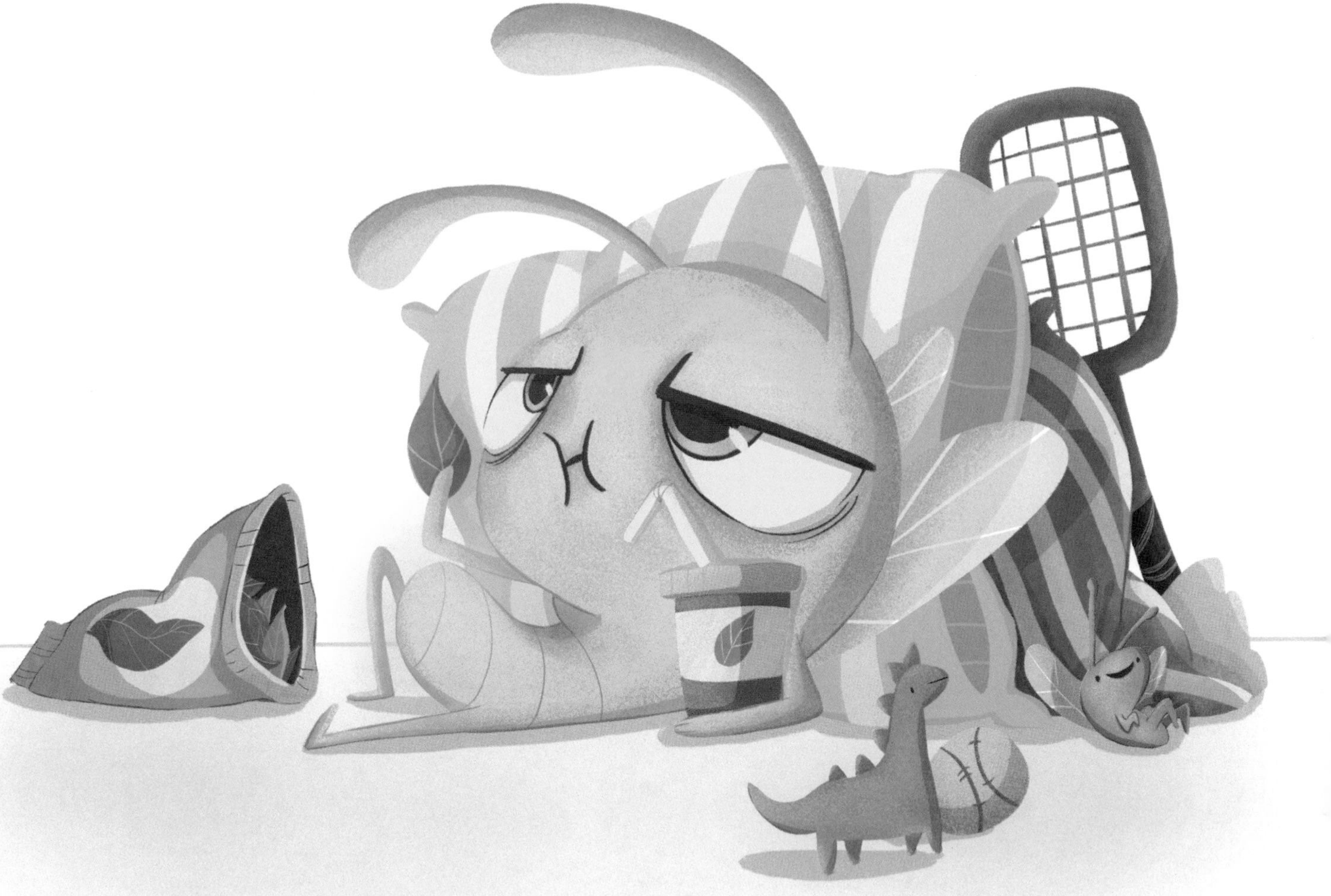

Bug loves doing nothing.

The other bugs look at him and say...

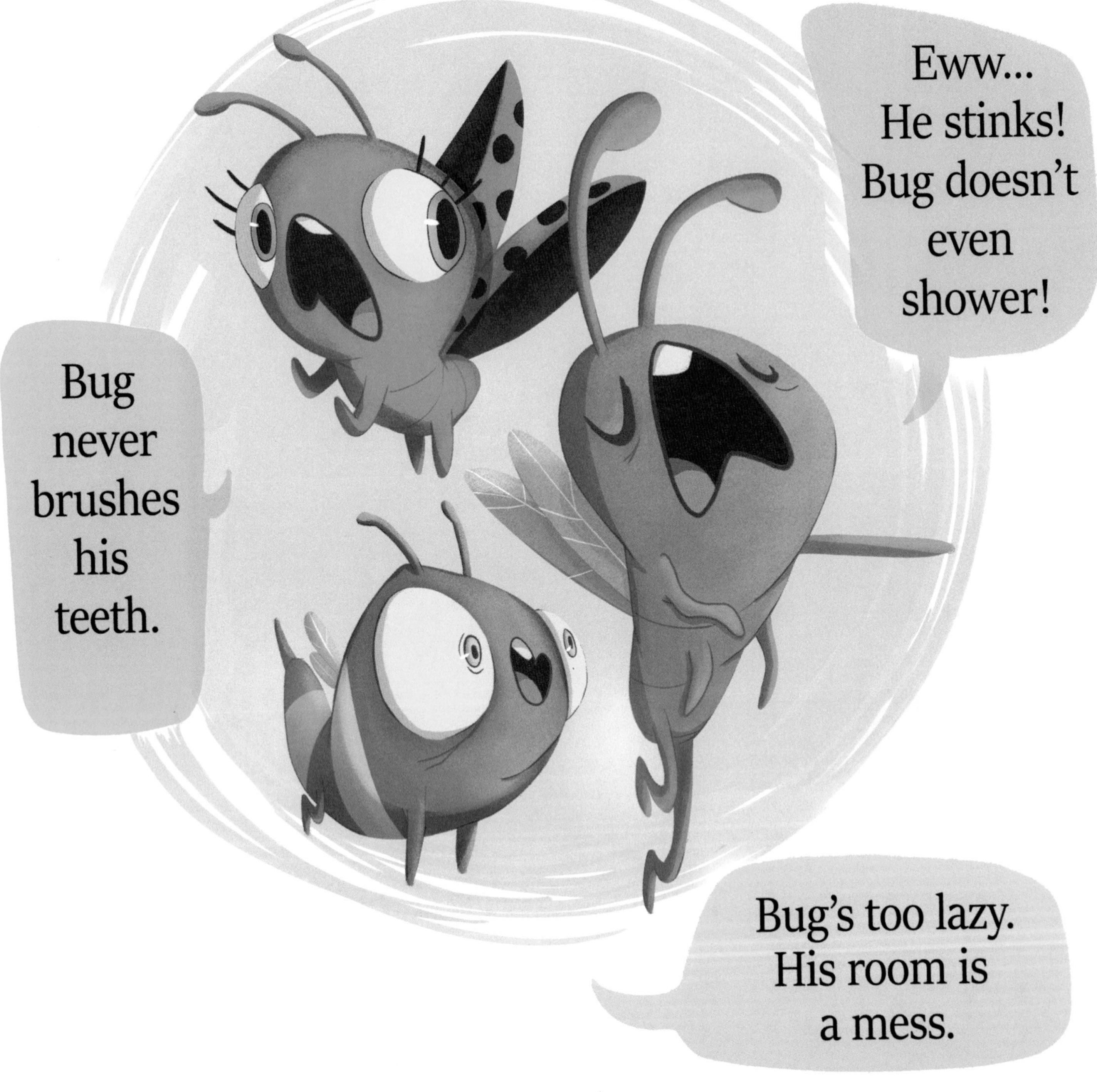
Eww... He stinks! Bug doesn't even shower!
Bug never brushes his teeth.
Bug's too lazy. His room is a mess.

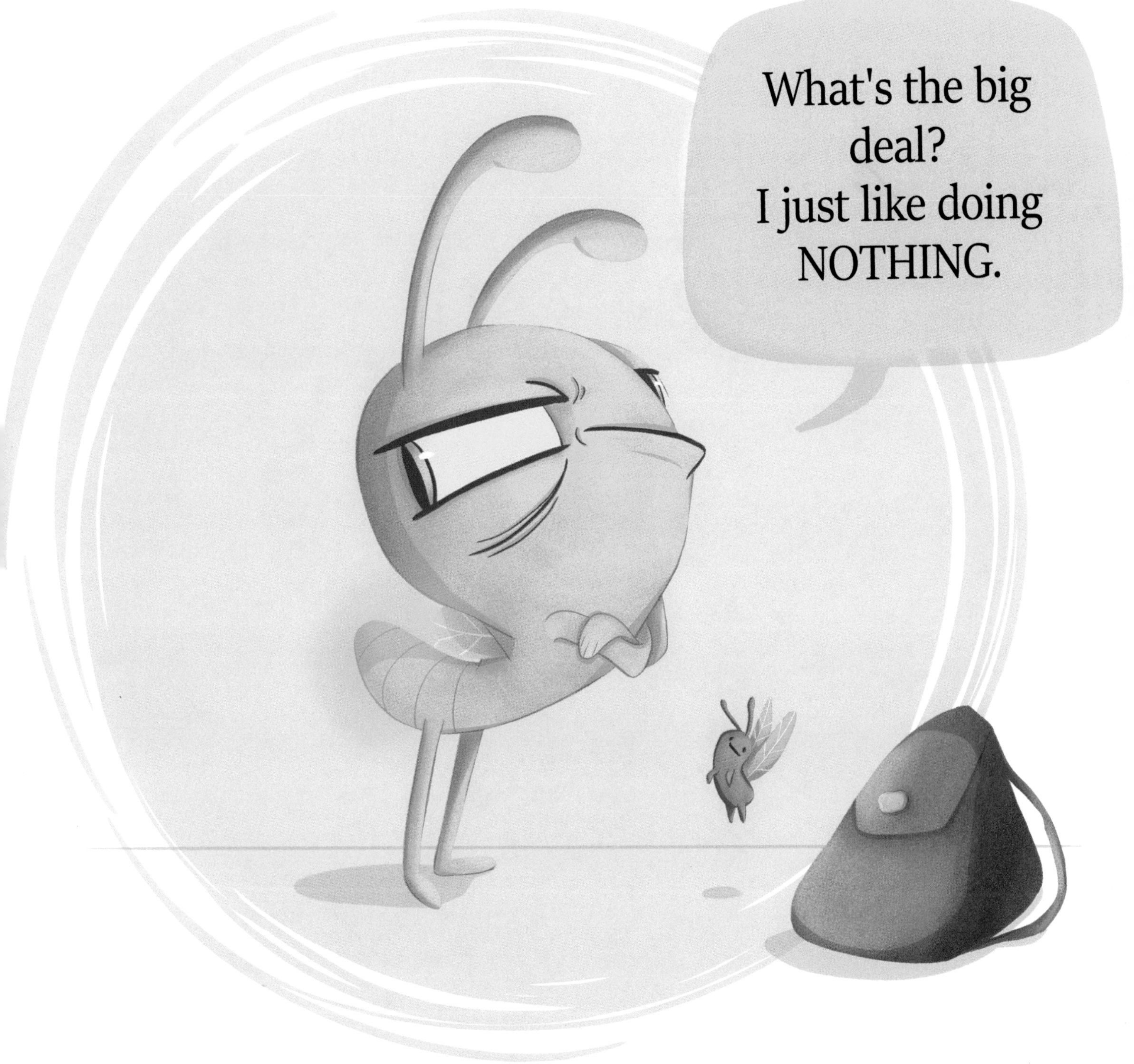
What's the big deal?
I just like doing NOTHING.

Every morning...

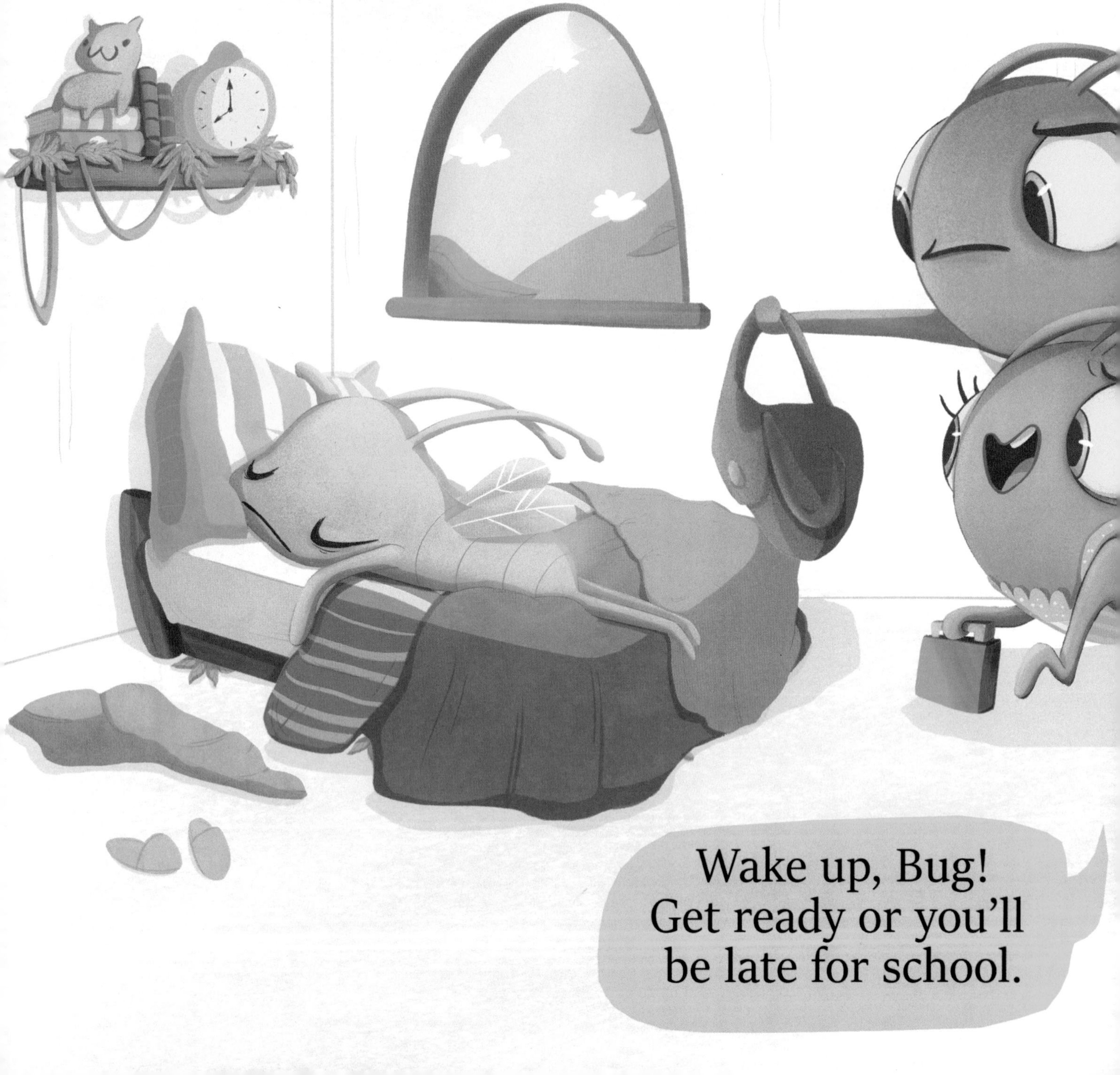
Wake up, Bug!
Get ready or you'll
be late for school.

Bug is always late for school.

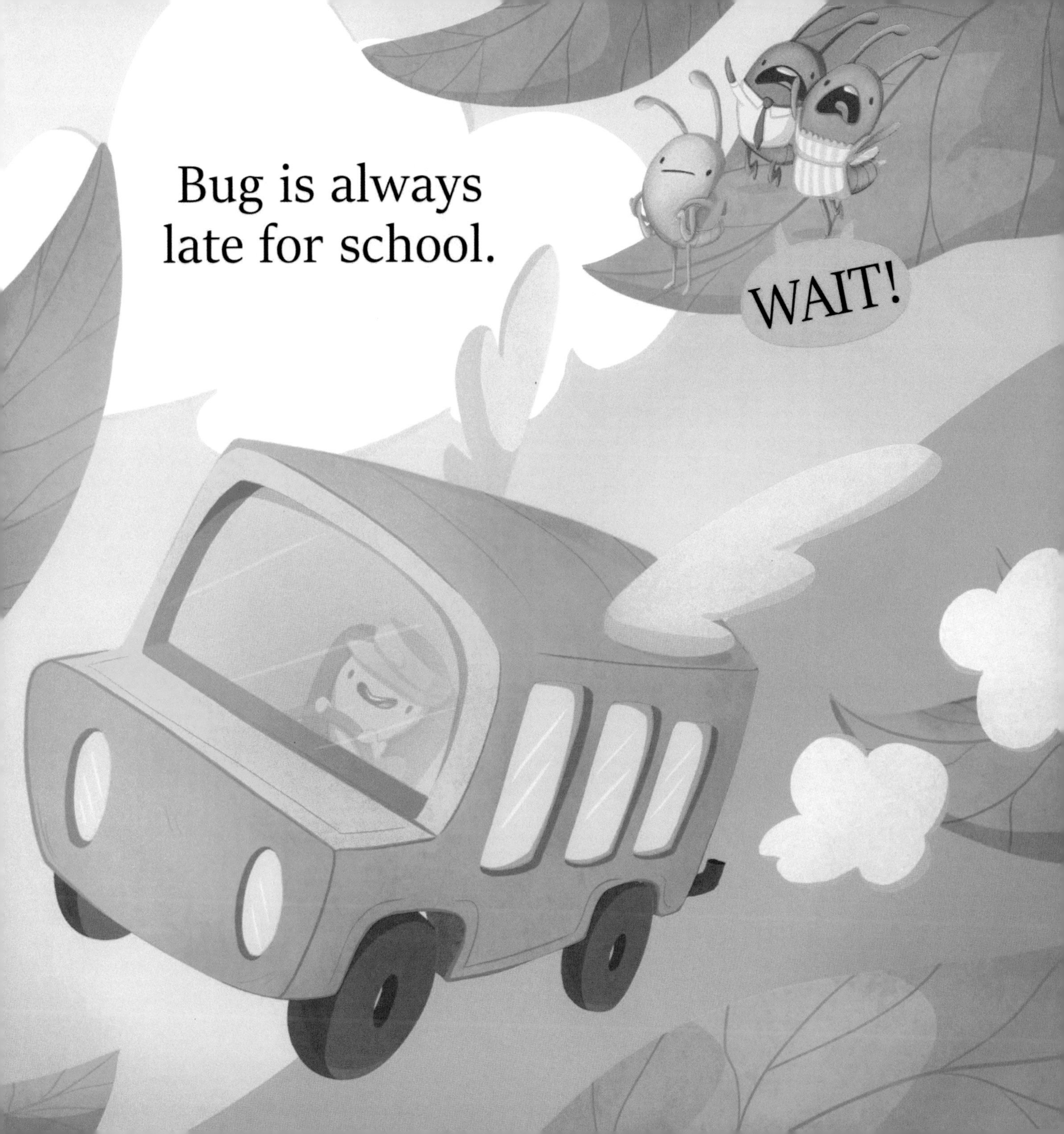
WAIT!

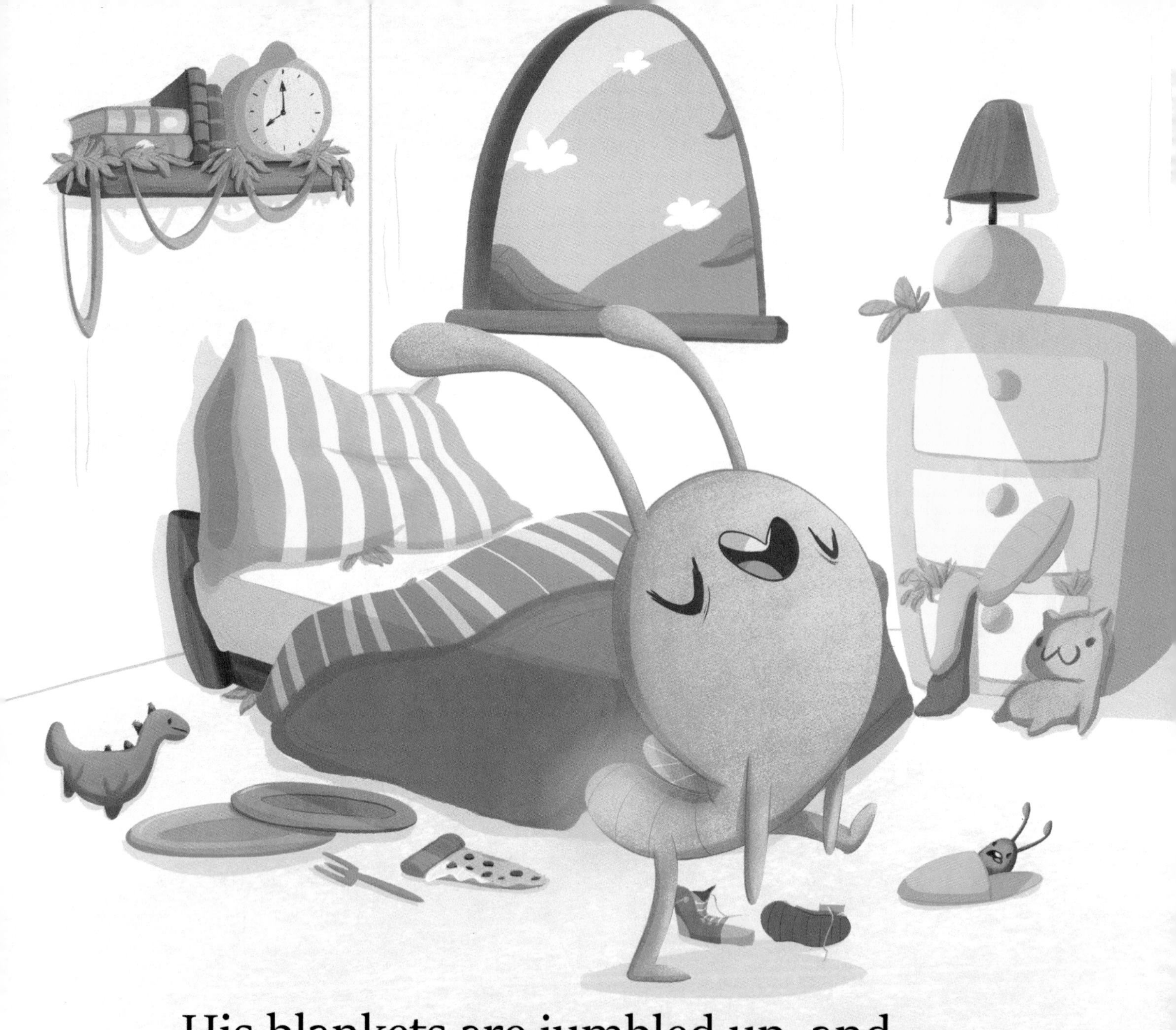

His blankets are jumbled up, and
he trips over his shoes every day.

He has a mountain of
toys in his room.

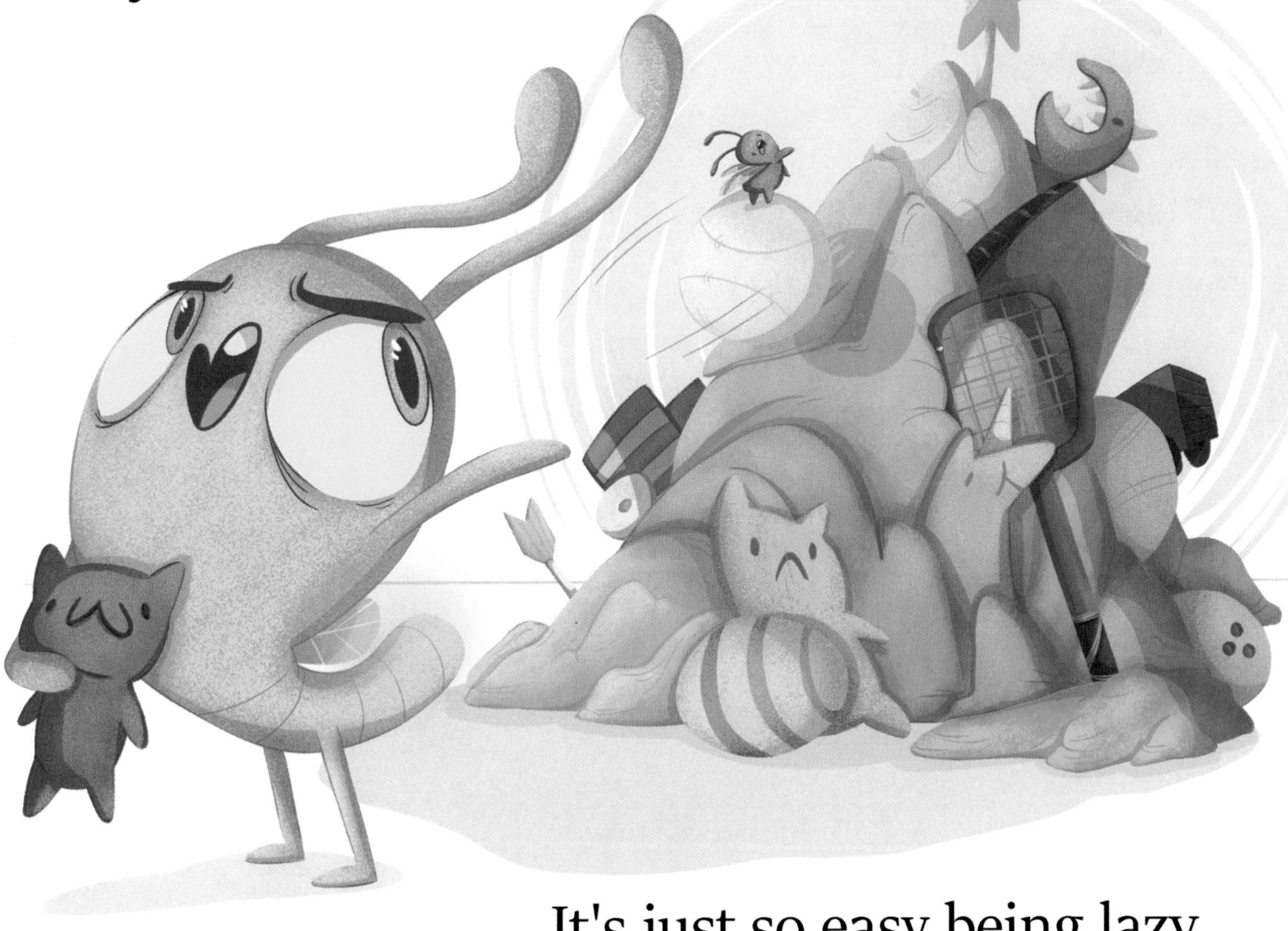

It's just so easy being lazy.

Mommy and Daddy worry about Bug.
They want him to be independent.

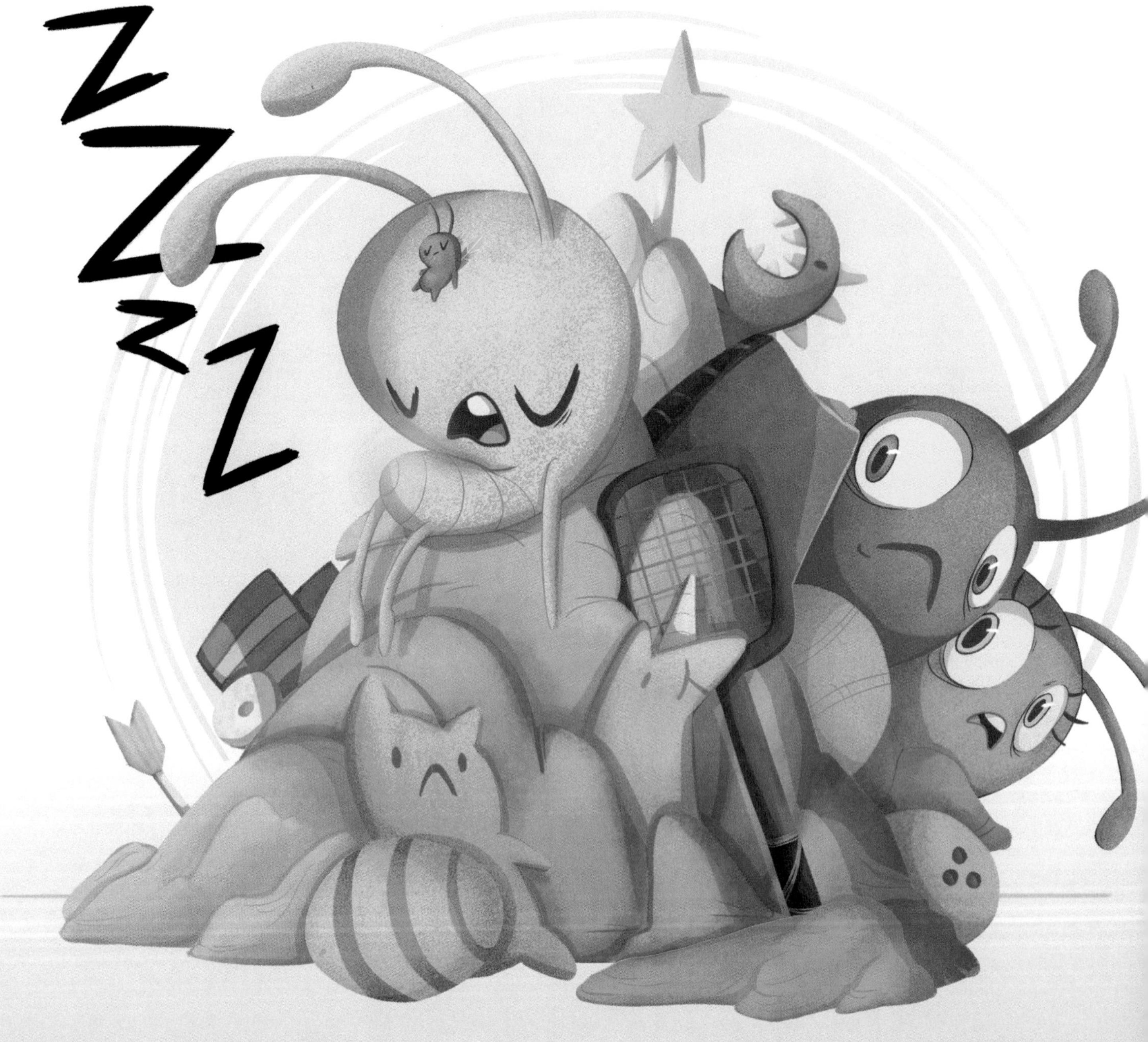

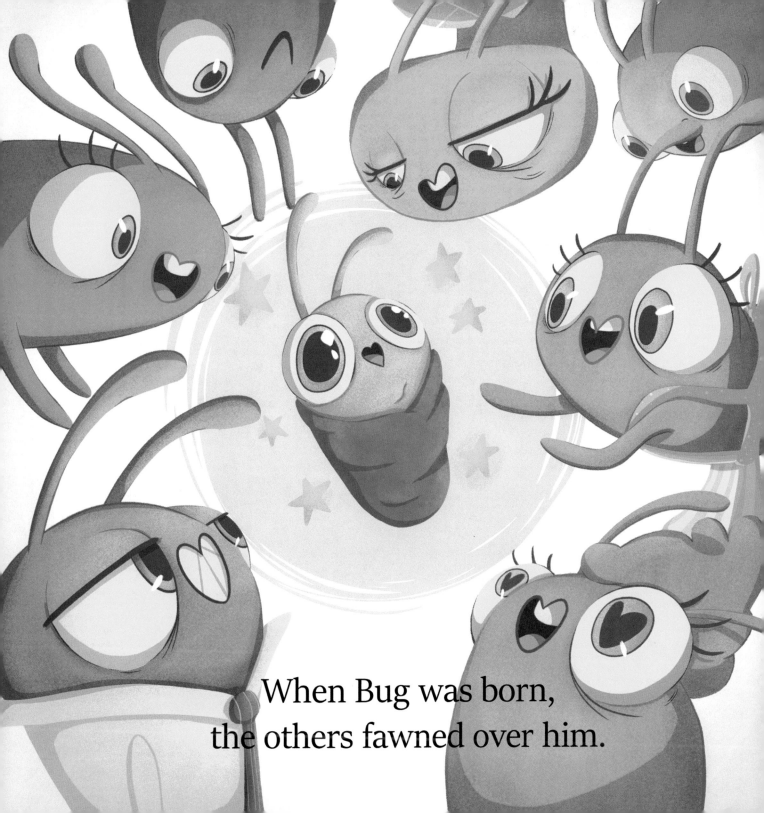

When Bug was born,
the others fawned over him.

They fed him, dressed him, made his bed and picked up his toys.

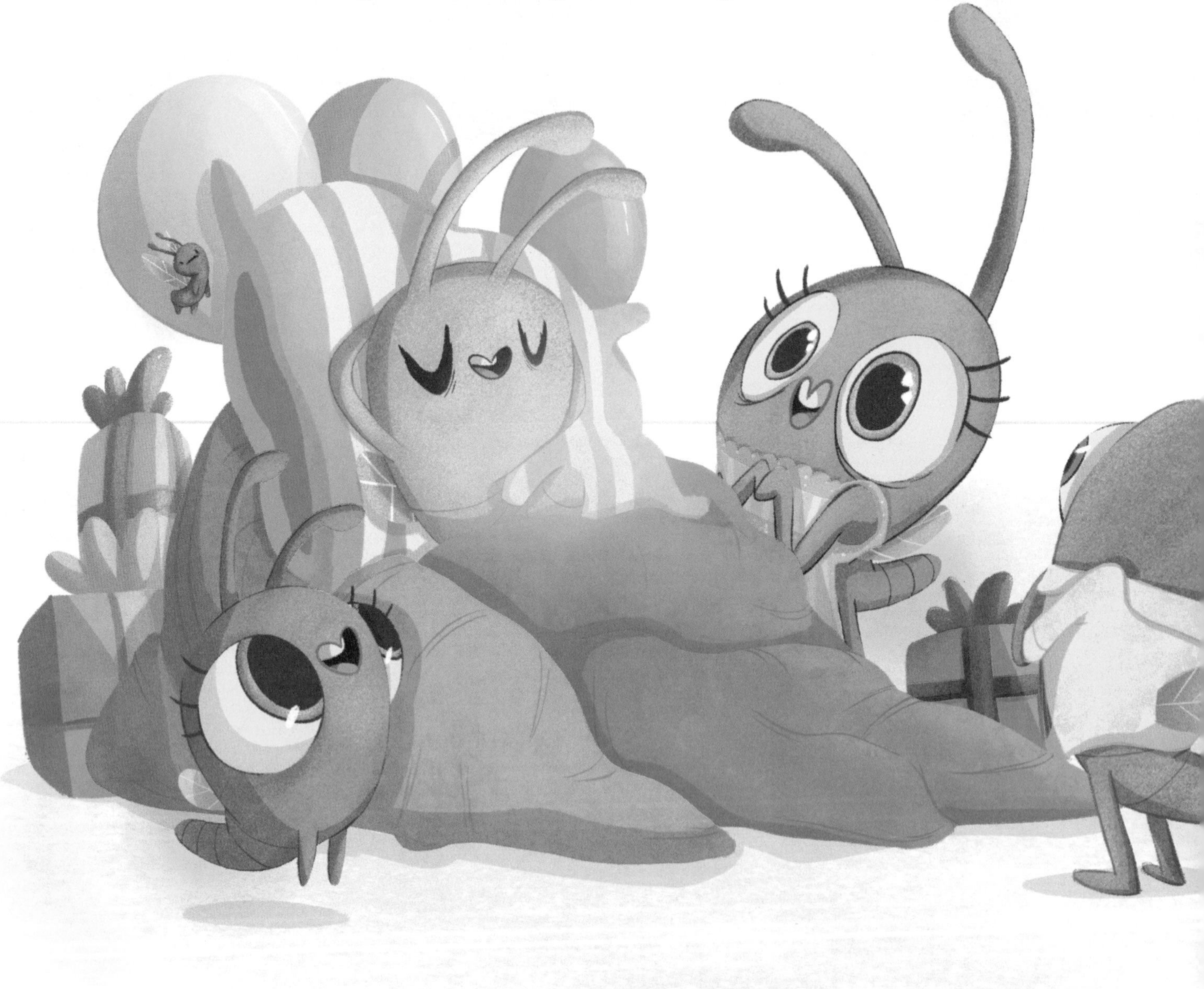

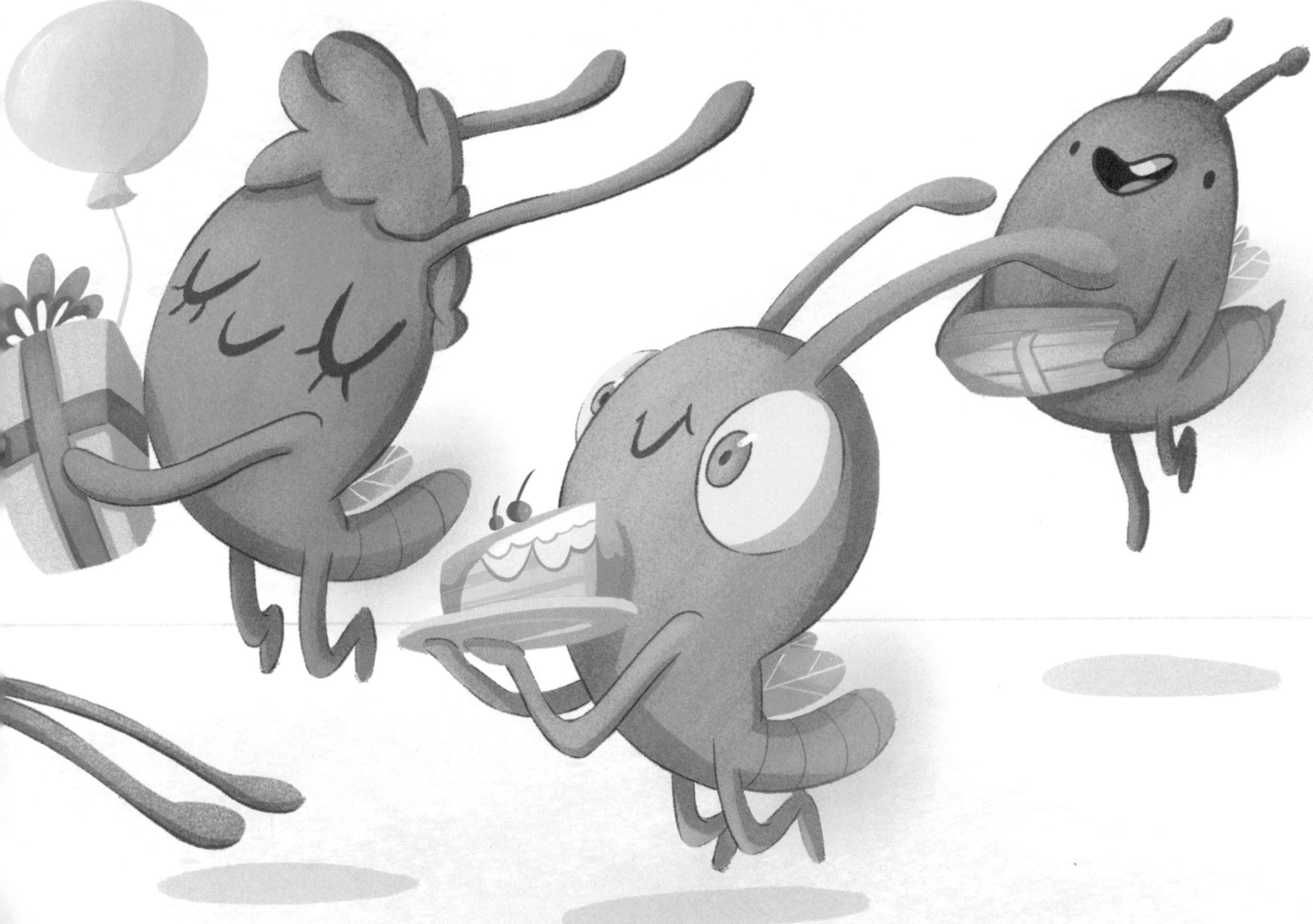

Bug liked when
others did things for him.

Now, even though he's big, he doesn't want to grow up and do Big Bug things.

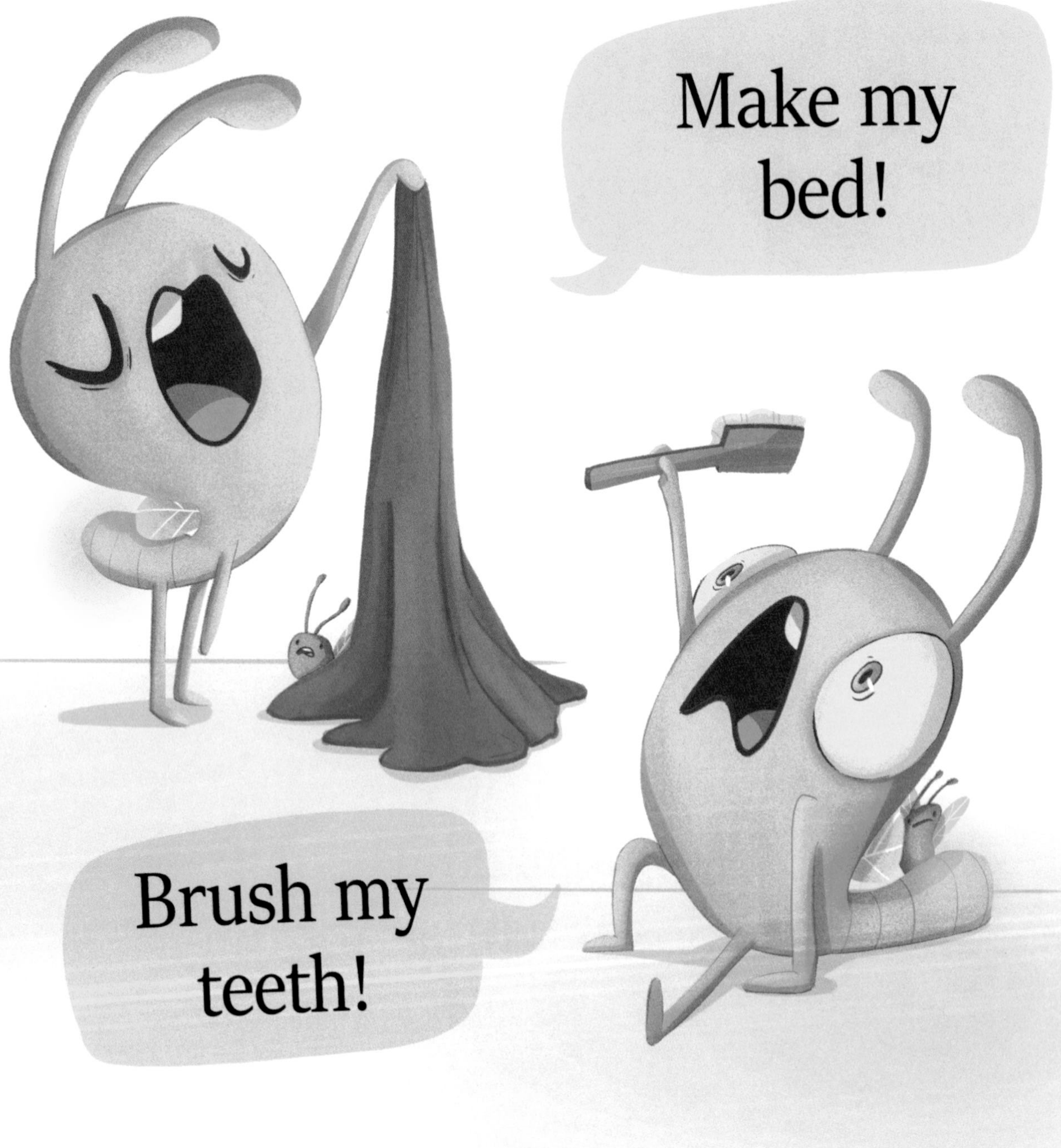
Make my bed!
Brush my teeth!

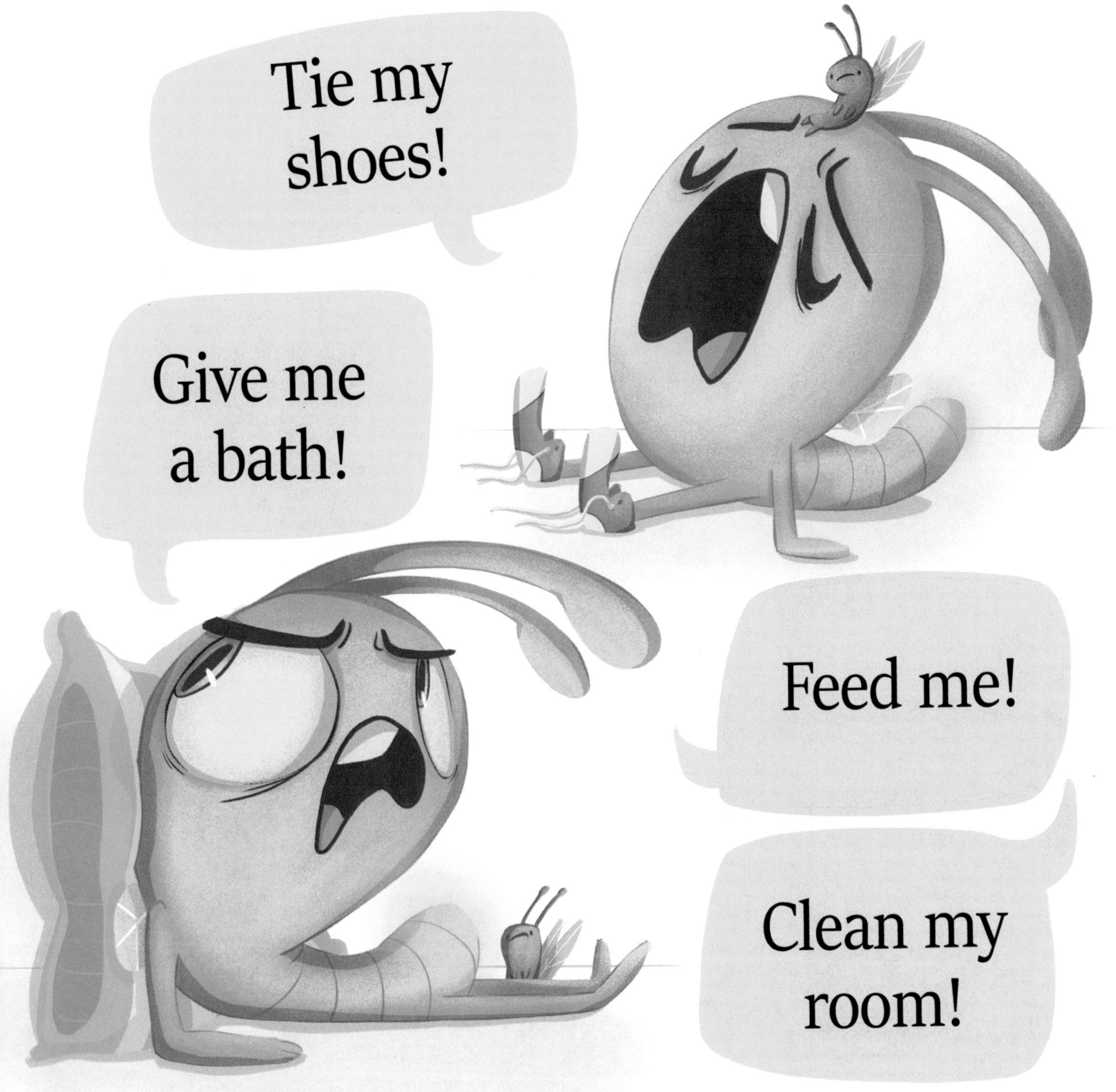
Tie my shoes!
Give me a bath!
Feed me!
Clean my room!

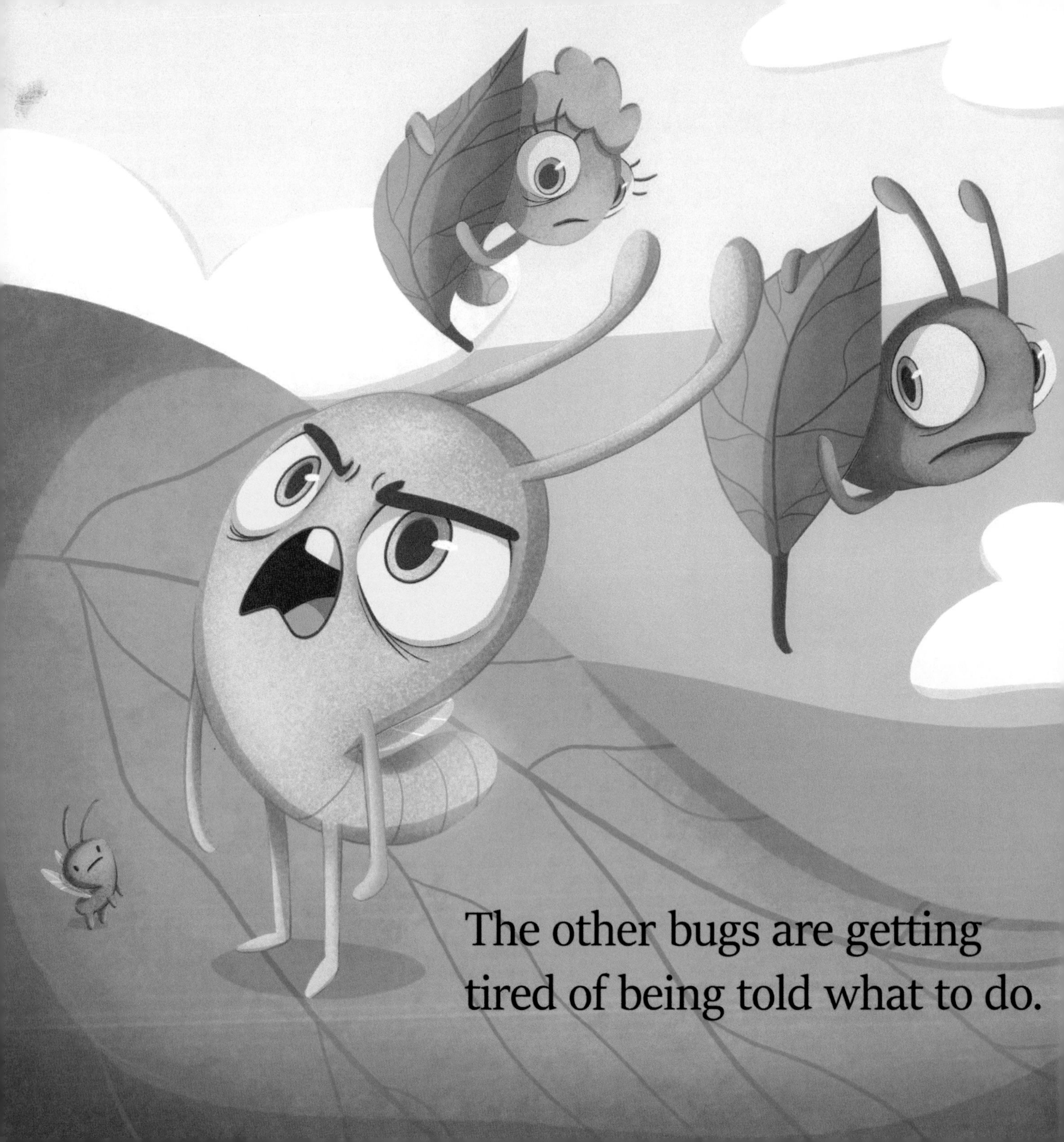

The other bugs are getting
tired of being told what to do.

One day Mommy and Daddy decide enough is enough...

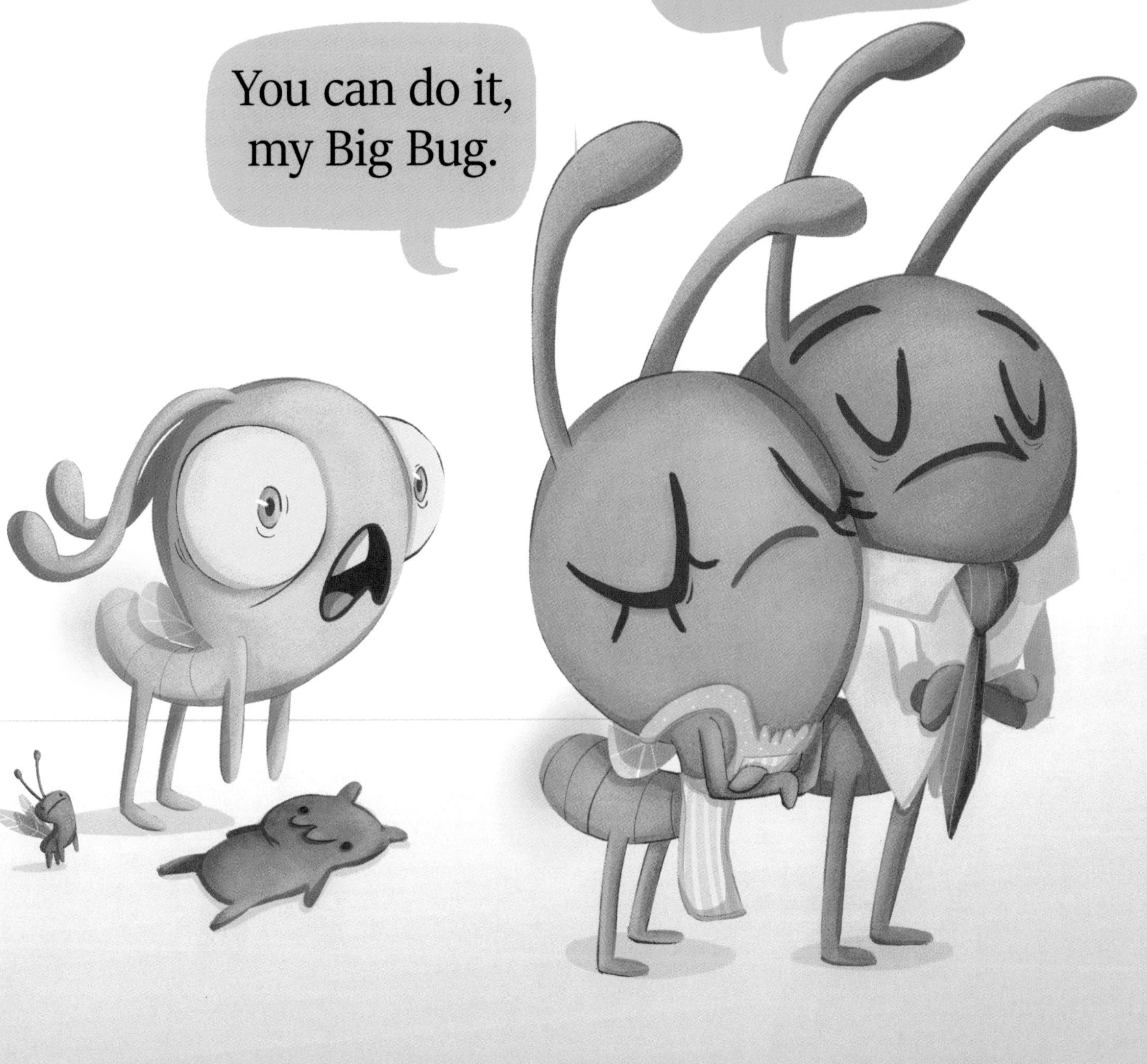
We love you, but no more being lazy.
You can do it, my Big Bug.

He screams and he shouts...

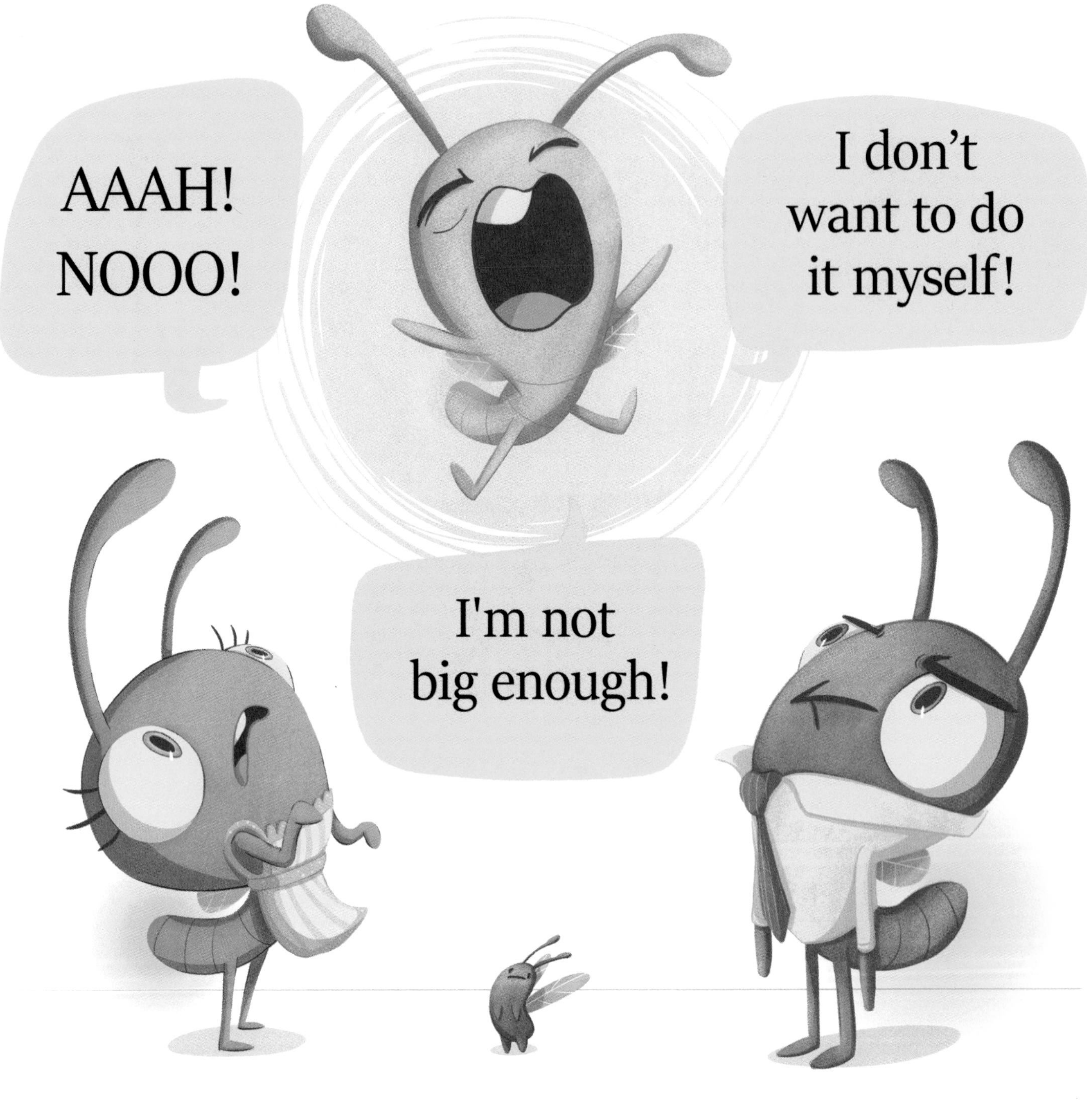
AAAH!
NOOO!
I don't
want to do
it myself!
I'm not
big enough!

The next morning, no one comes to dress Bug.

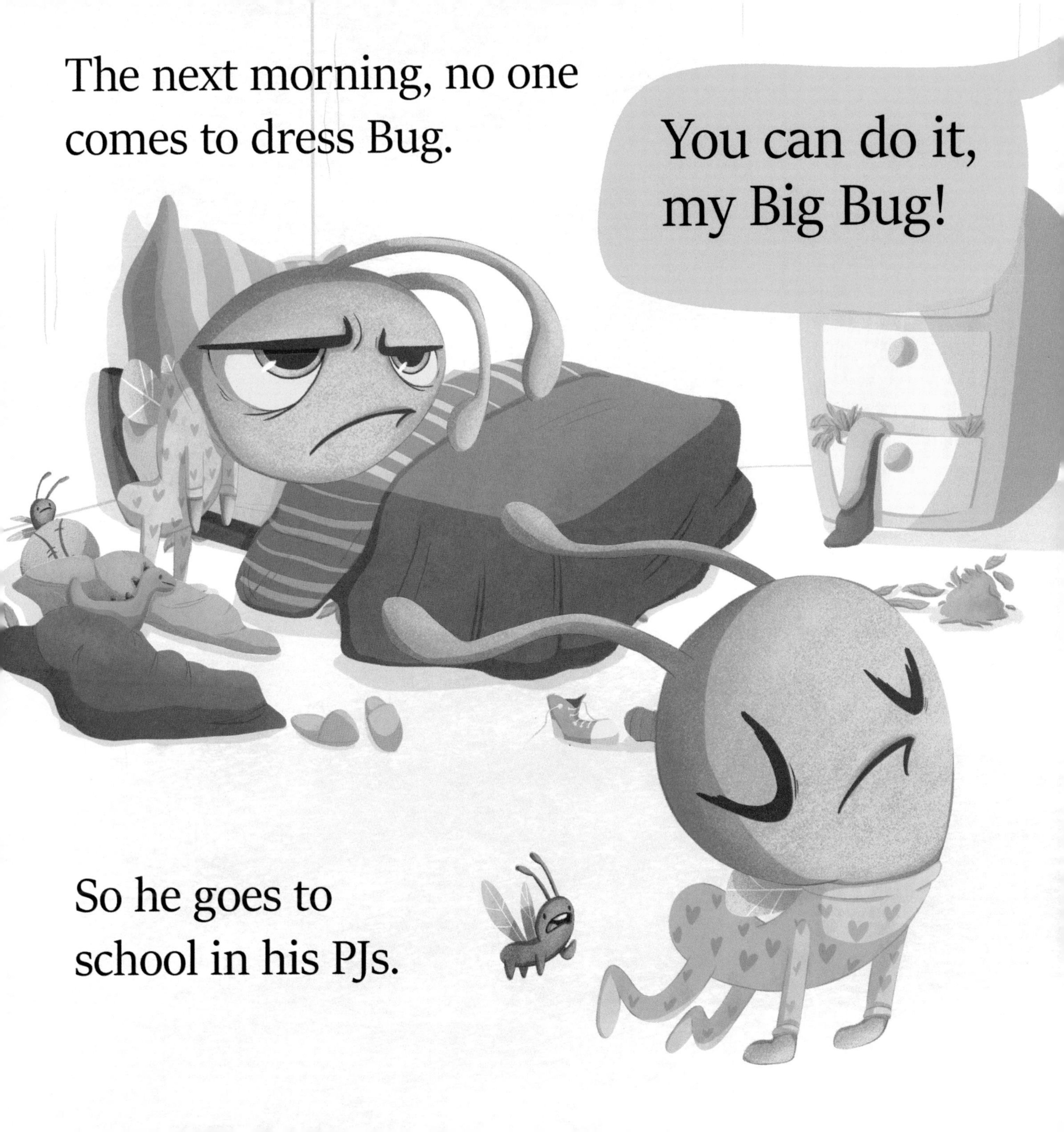
You can do it, my Big Bug!

So he goes to school in his PJs.

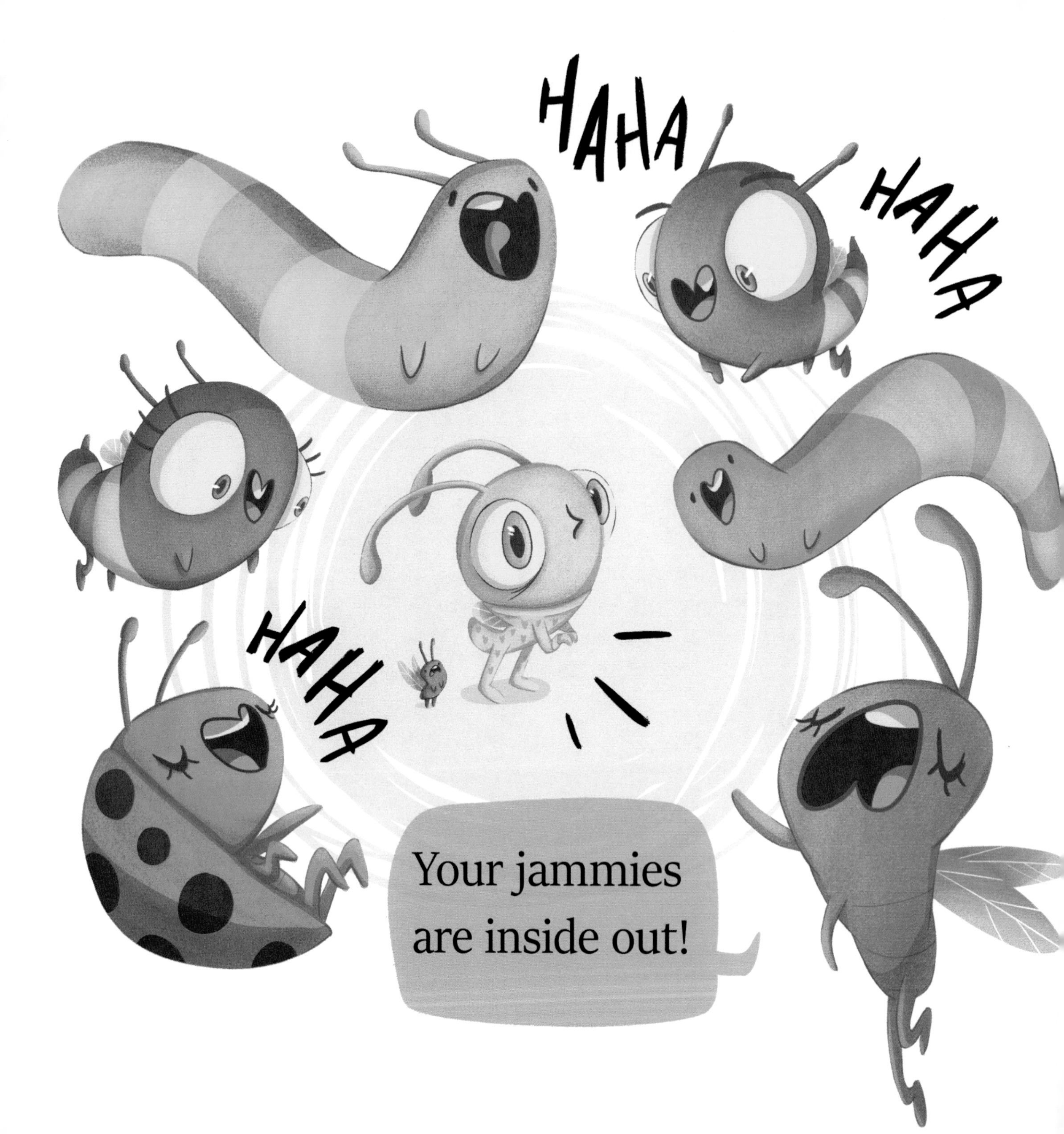
HAHA
HAHA
HAHA
Your jammies are inside out!

The teacher says...

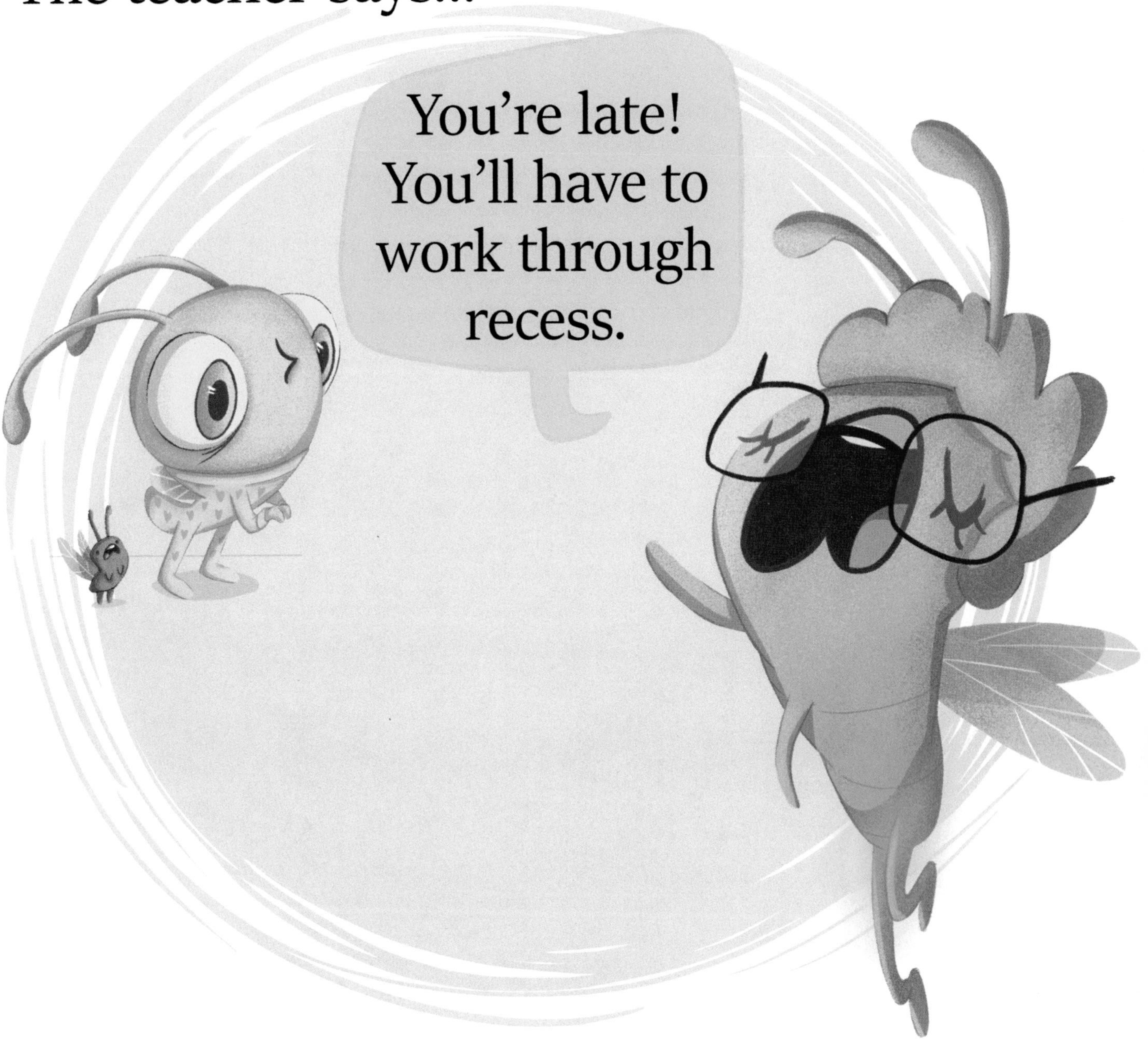
You're late! You'll have to work through recess.

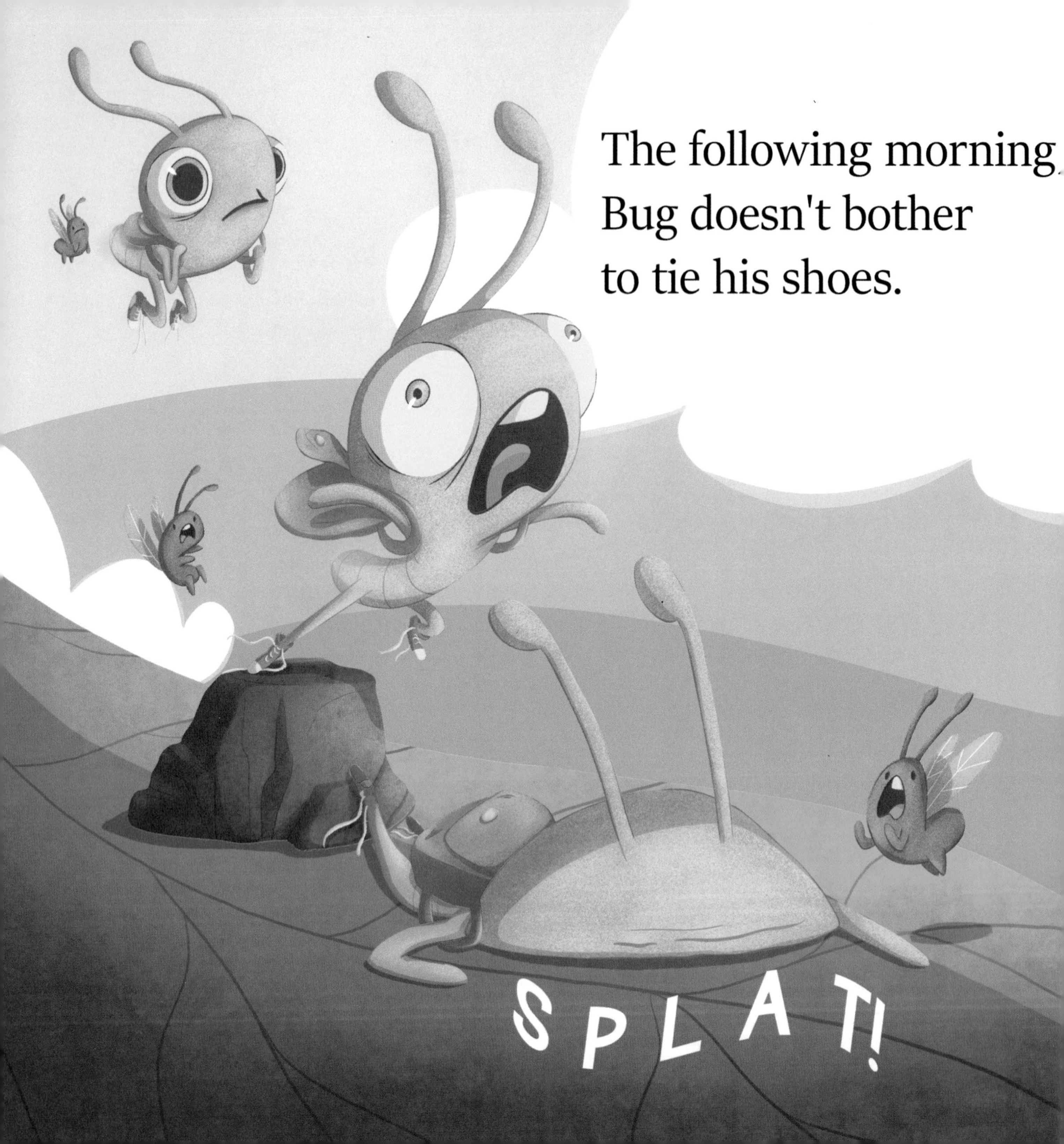
The following morning,
Bug doesn't bother
to tie his shoes.
SPLAT!

The doctor says...

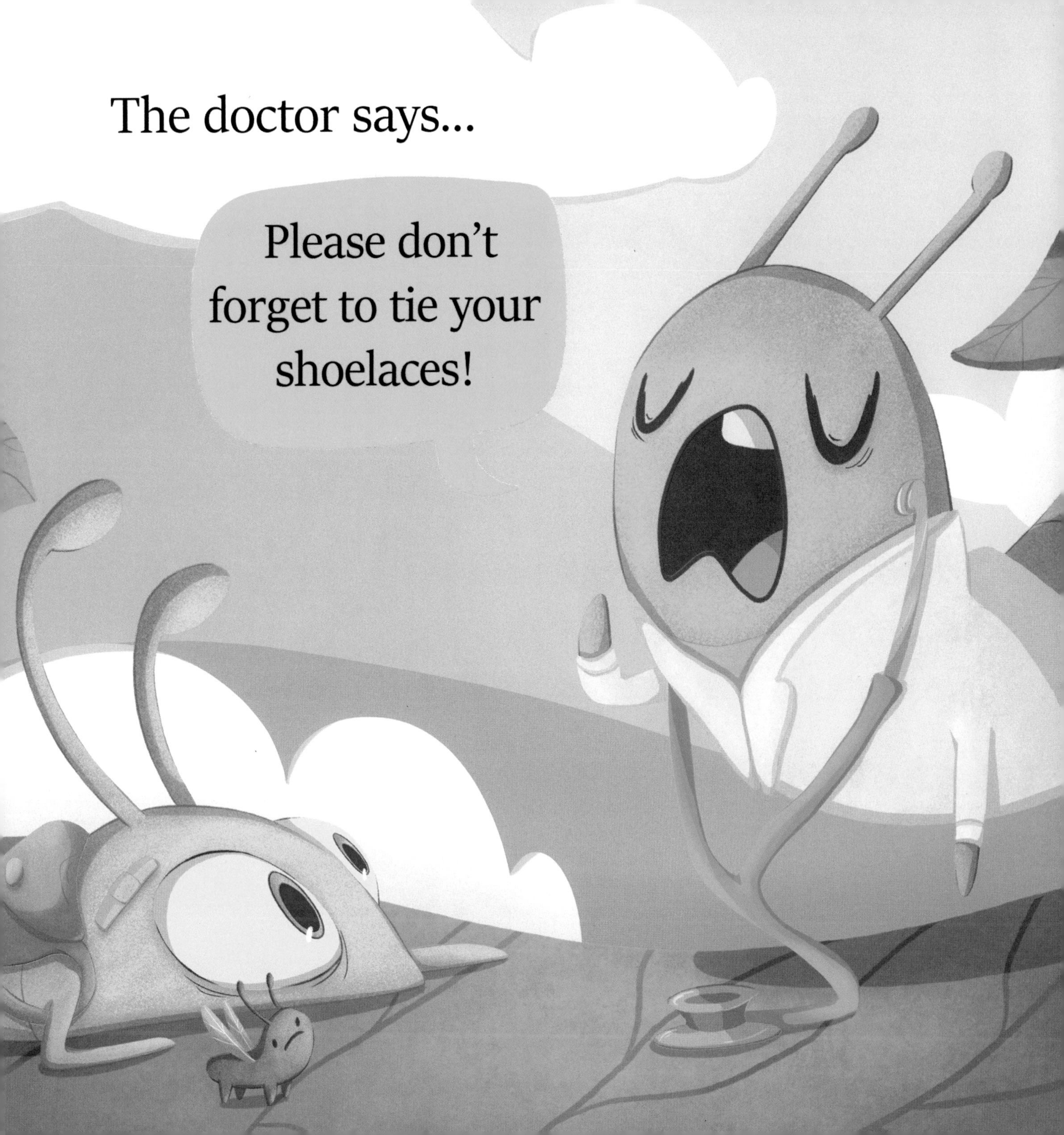
Please don't forget to tie your shoelaces!

After school
Bug yells...

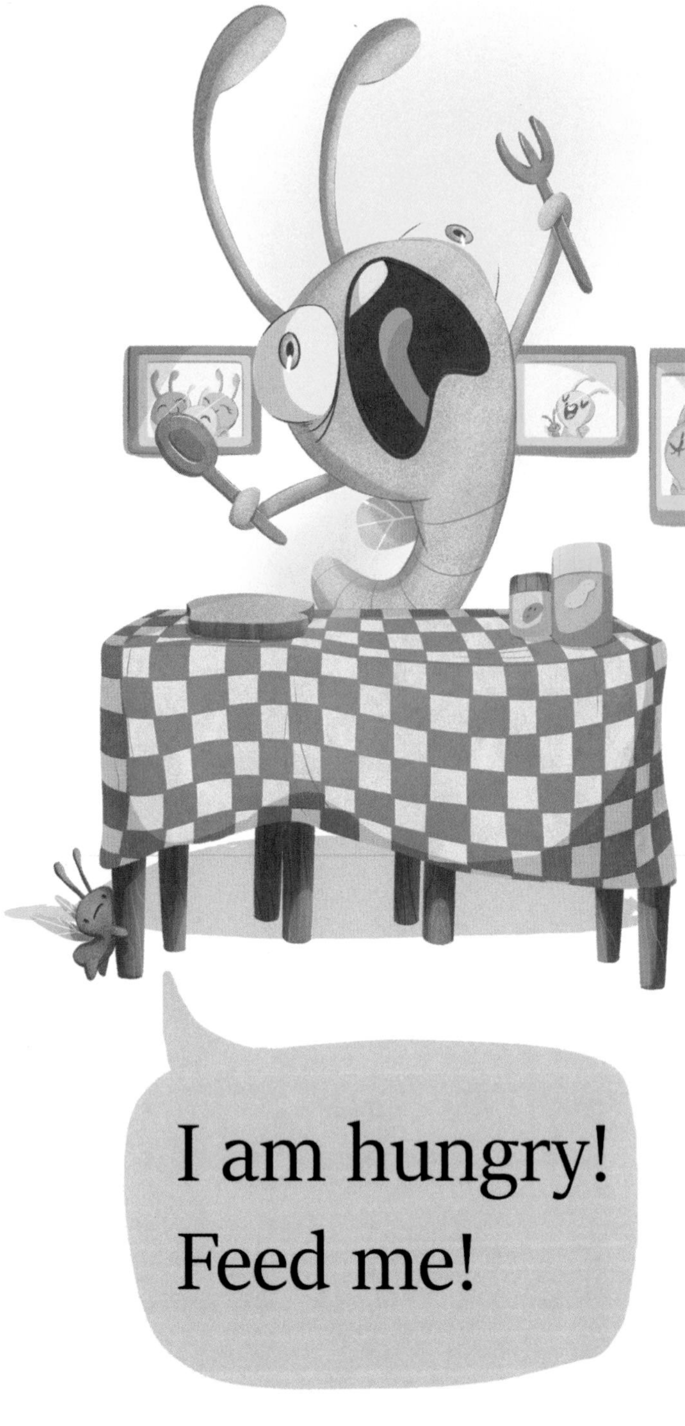
I am hungry!
Feed me!

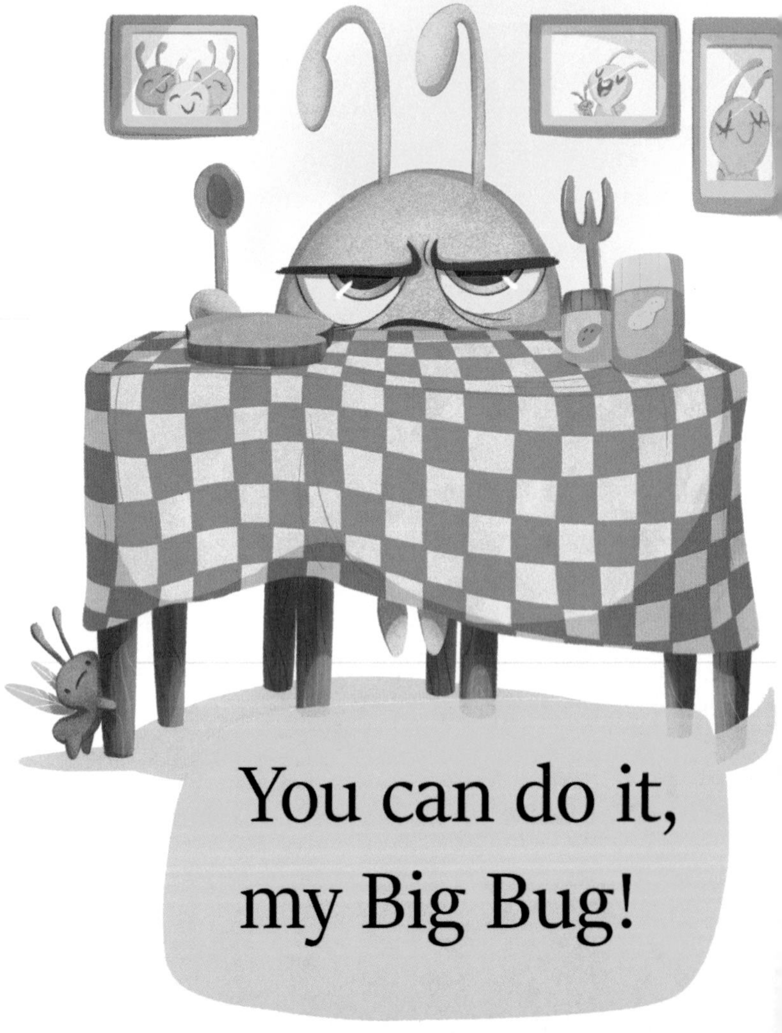
You can do it,
my Big Bug!

Bug sulks in his room.

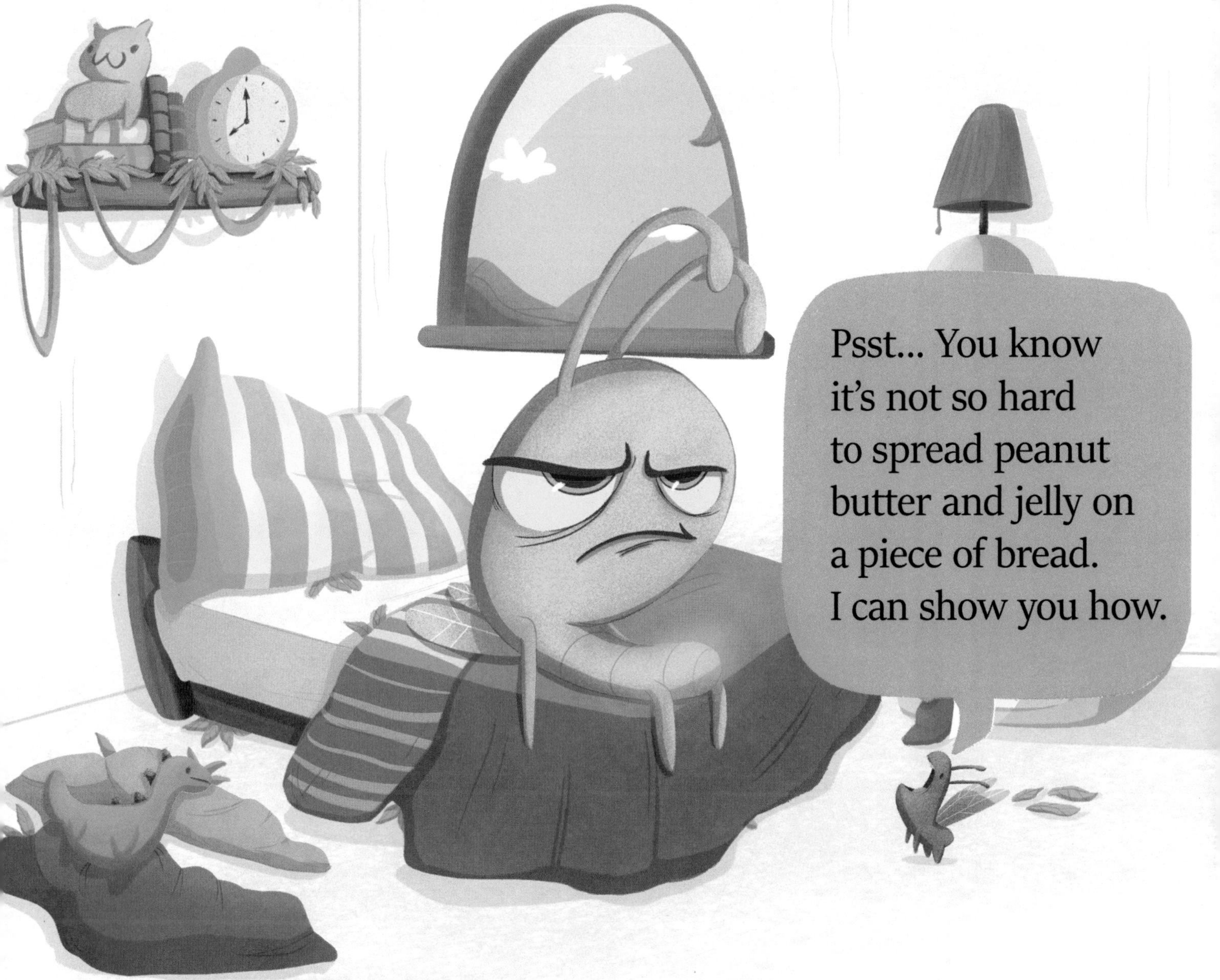
Psst... You know it's not so hard to spread peanut butter and jelly on a piece of bread. I can show you how.

His stomach growls, so...

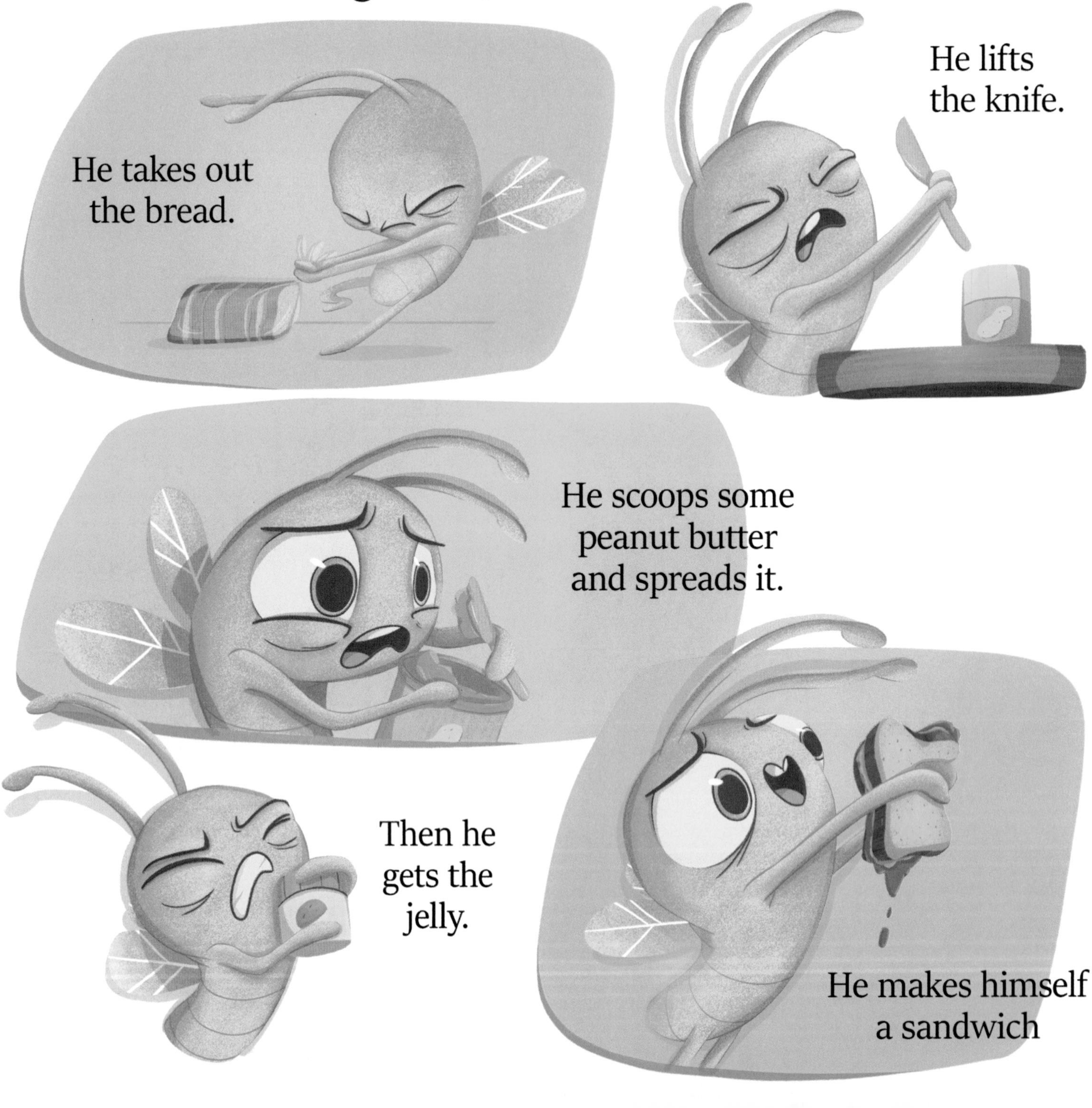

He takes out the bread.

He lifts the knife.

He scoops some peanut butter and spreads it.

Then he gets the jelly.

He makes himself a sandwich

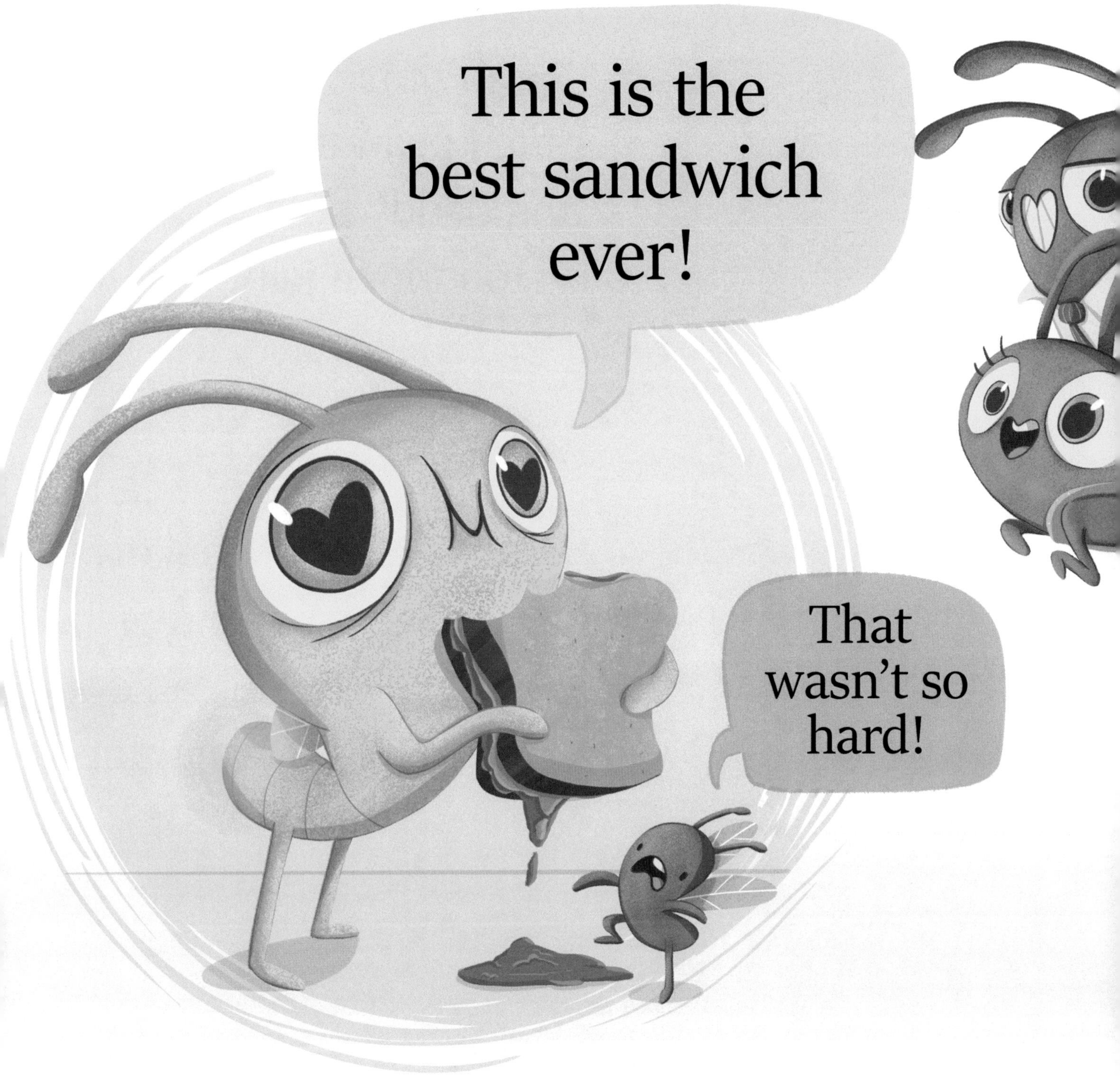
This is the best sandwich ever!
That wasn't so hard!

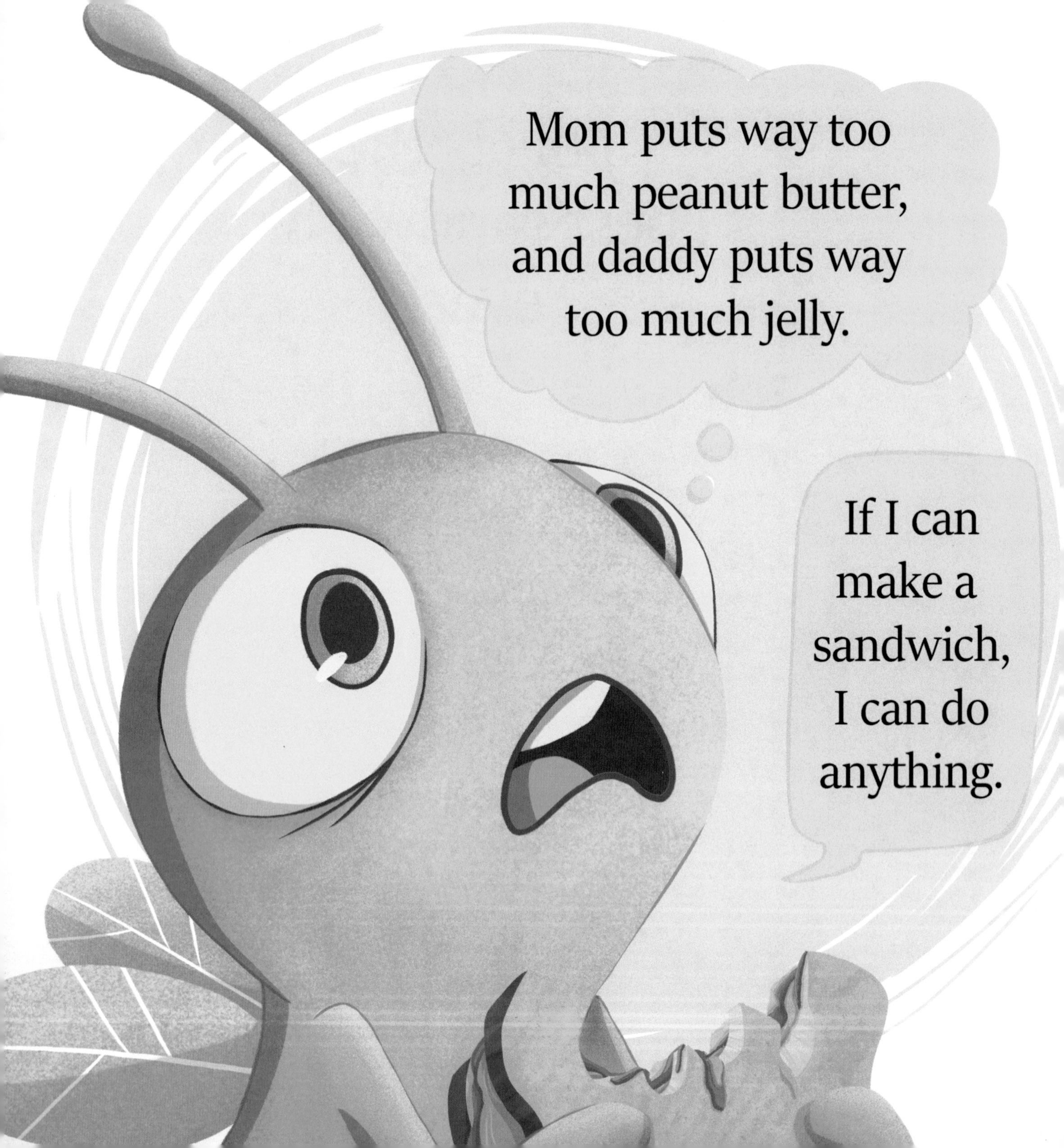
Mom puts way too much peanut butter, and daddy puts way too much jelly.
If I can make a sandwich, I can do anything.

Bug realizes he wants to change.

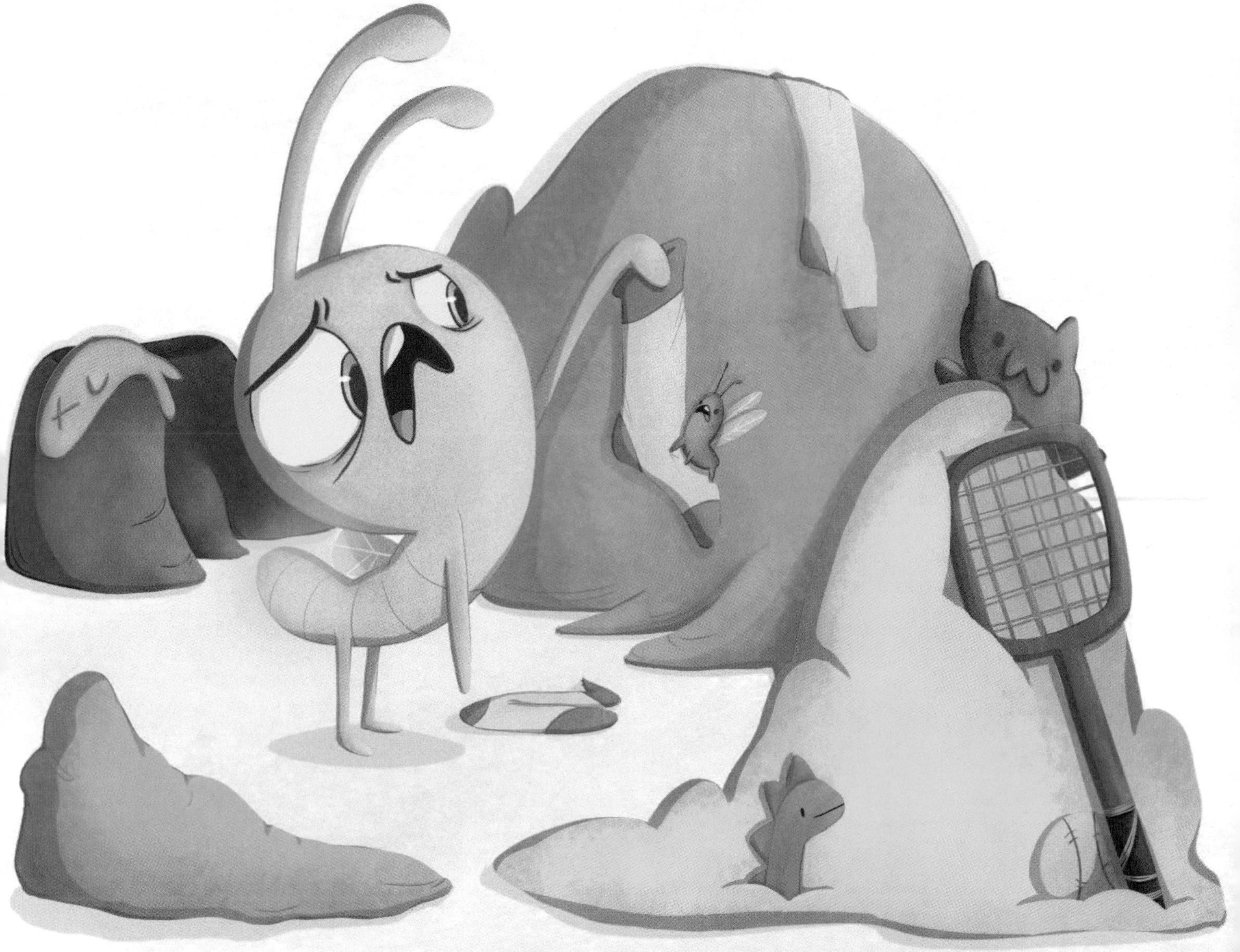

But change can be hard when you're used to doing nothing.

But, he is trying. He's taking baby steps.

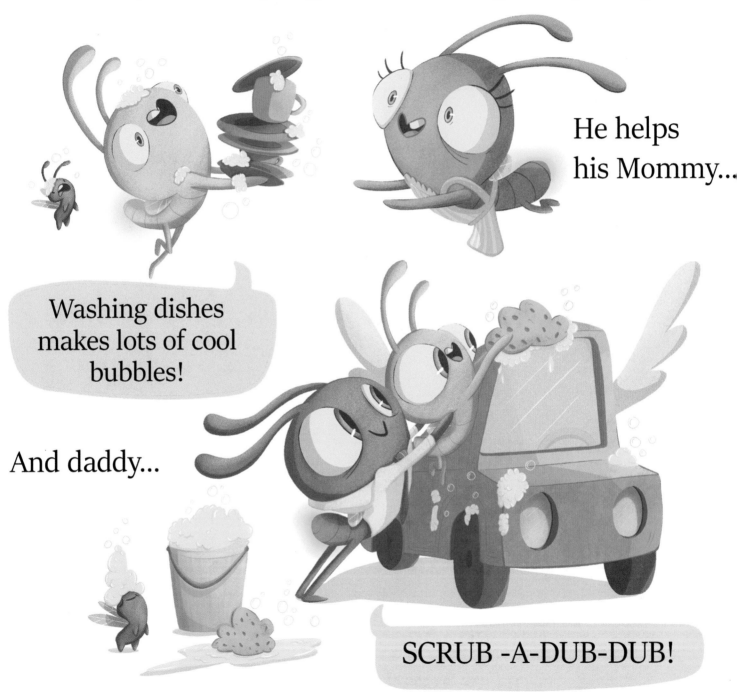

He helps
his Mommy...

Washing dishes
makes lots of cool
bubbles!

And daddy...

SCRUB -A-DUB-DUB!

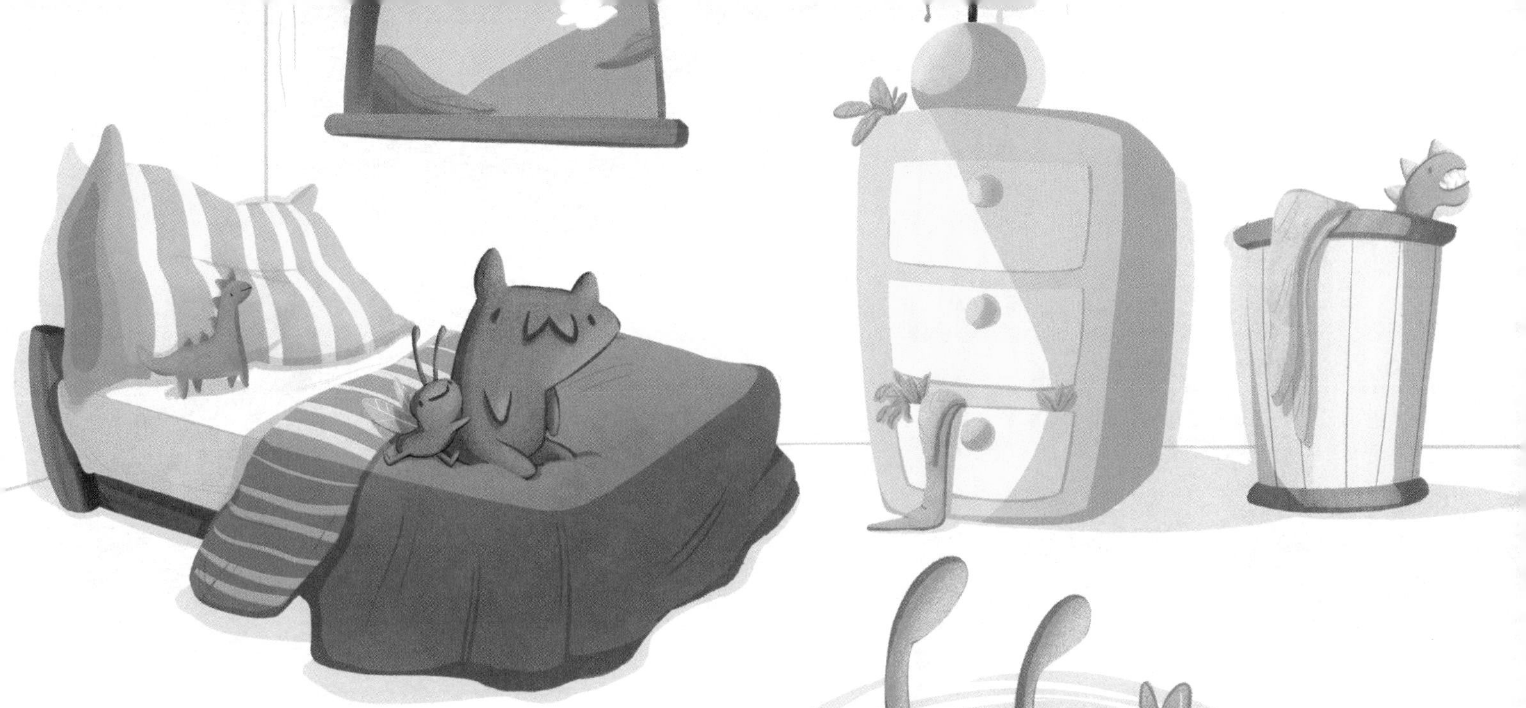

Sometimes, he still forgets to clean up his room, or make his bed.

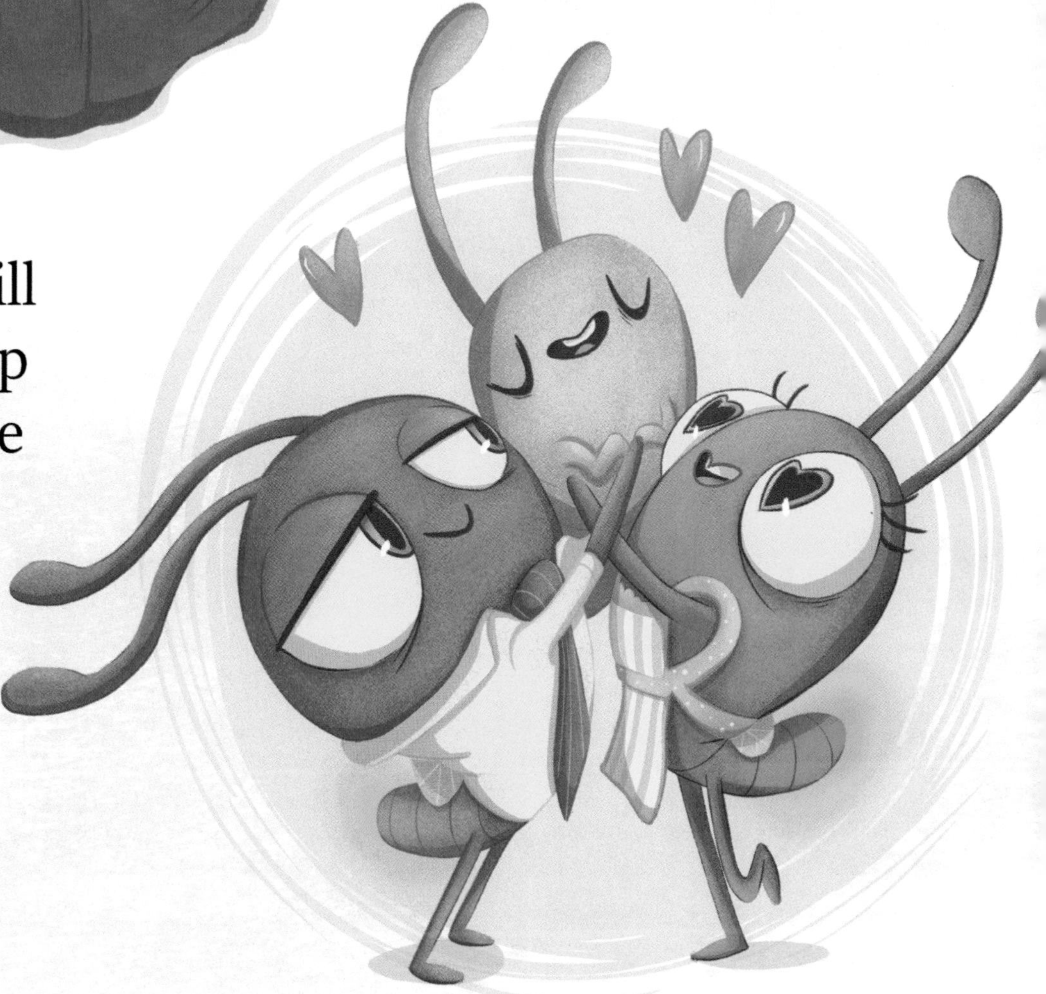

But he remembers to brush his teeth every day.

Sometimes he needs
to ask others for help,
but not all the time.

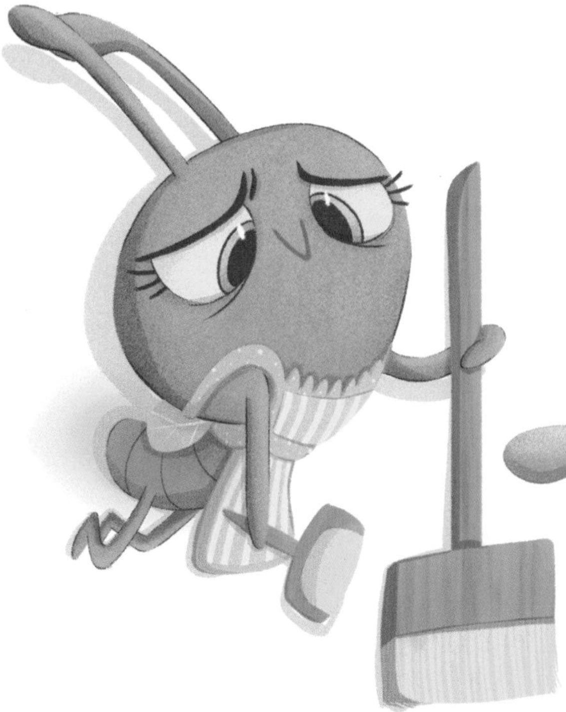

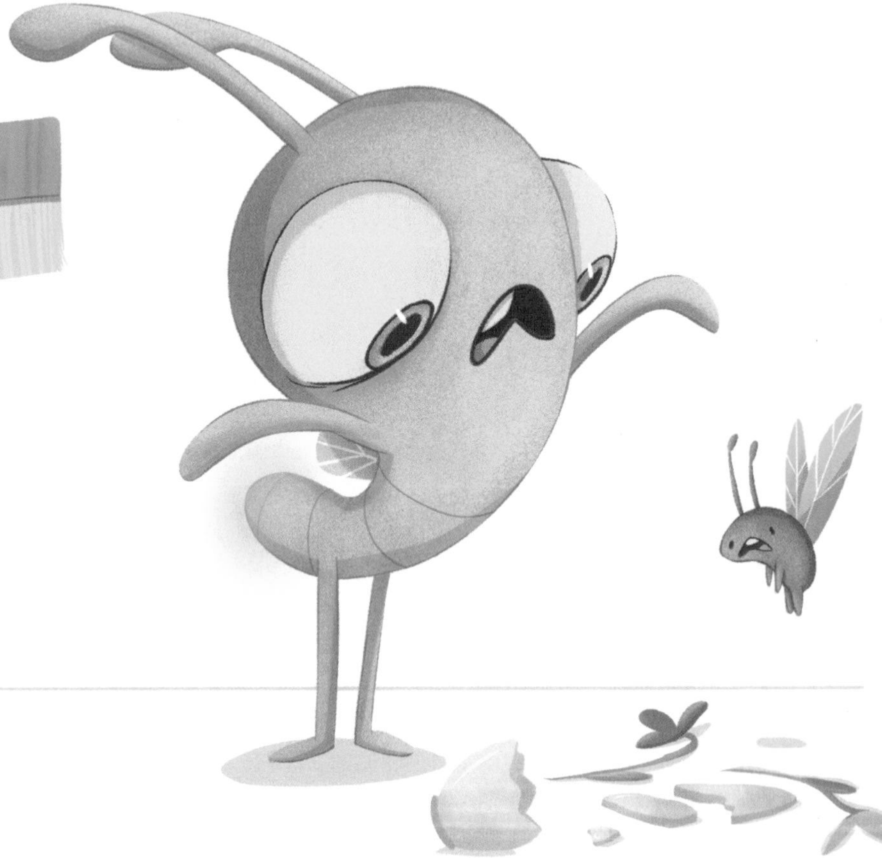

He is trying
his best.

Bug even makes sandwiches for his friends!

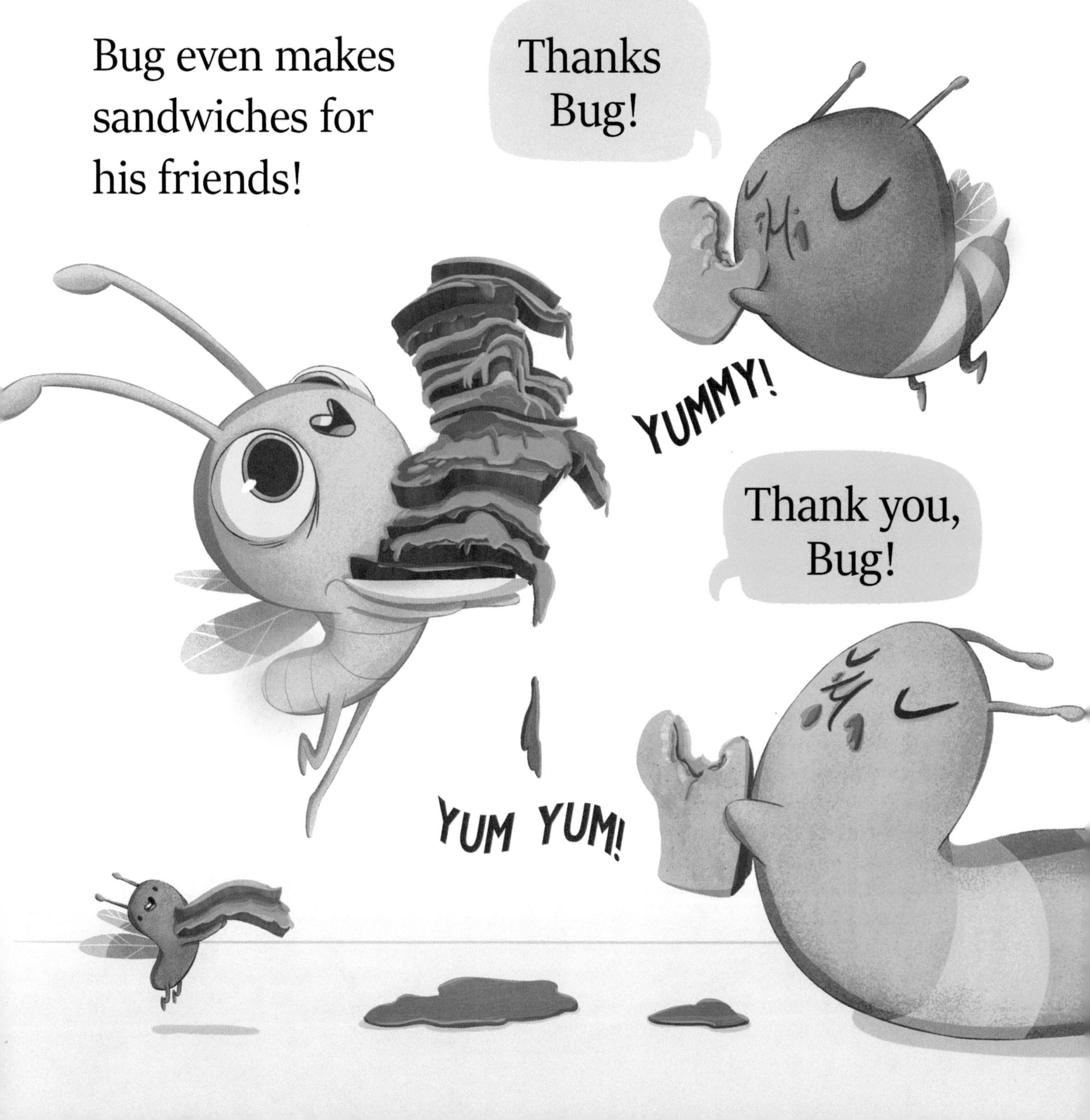
Thanks Bug!
YUMMY!
Thank you, Bug!
YUM YUM!

He's a can-do bug!

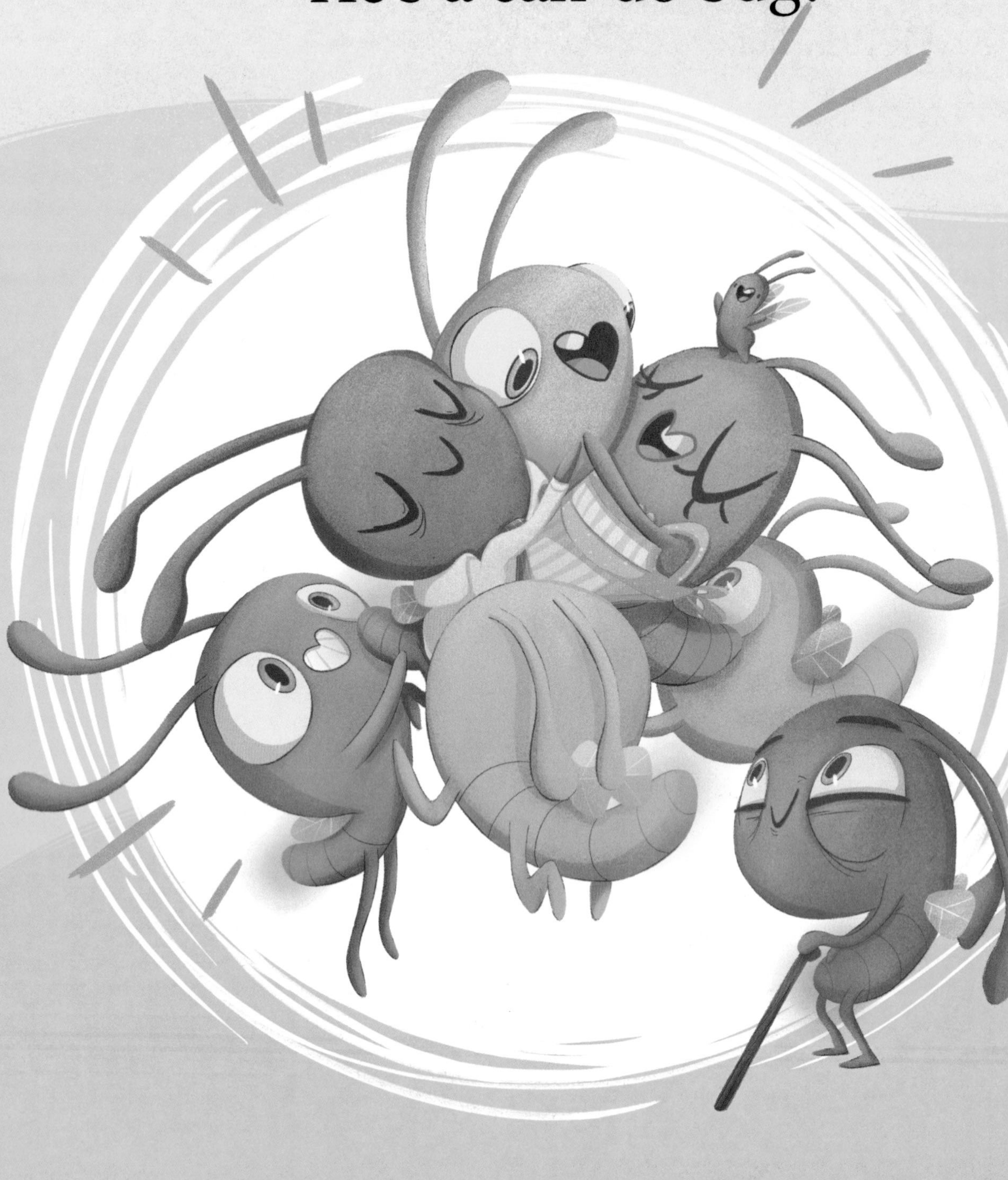

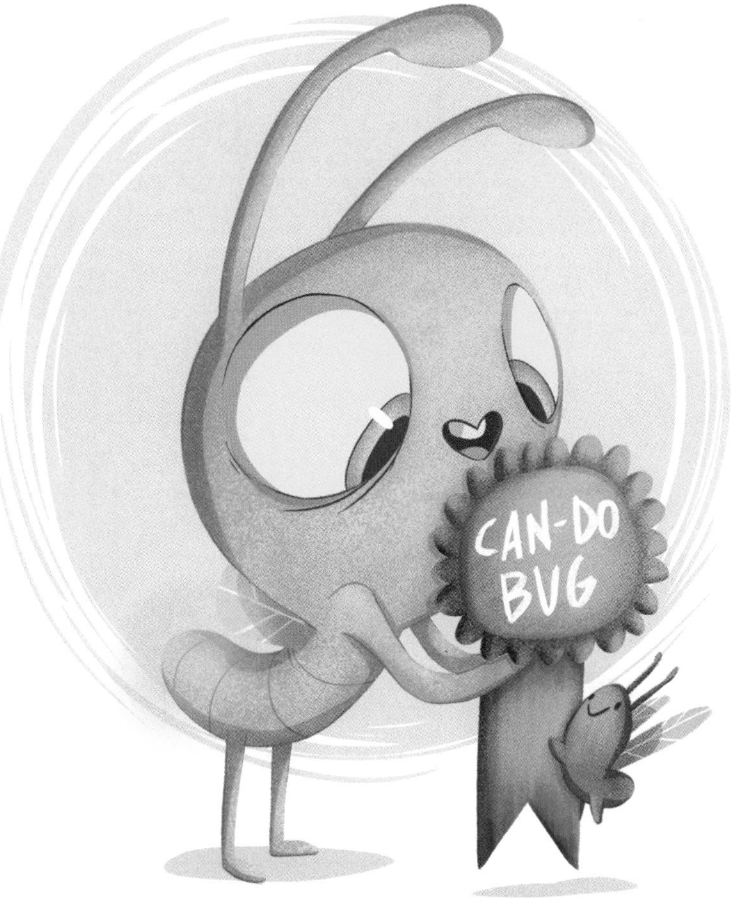
CAN-DO
BUG

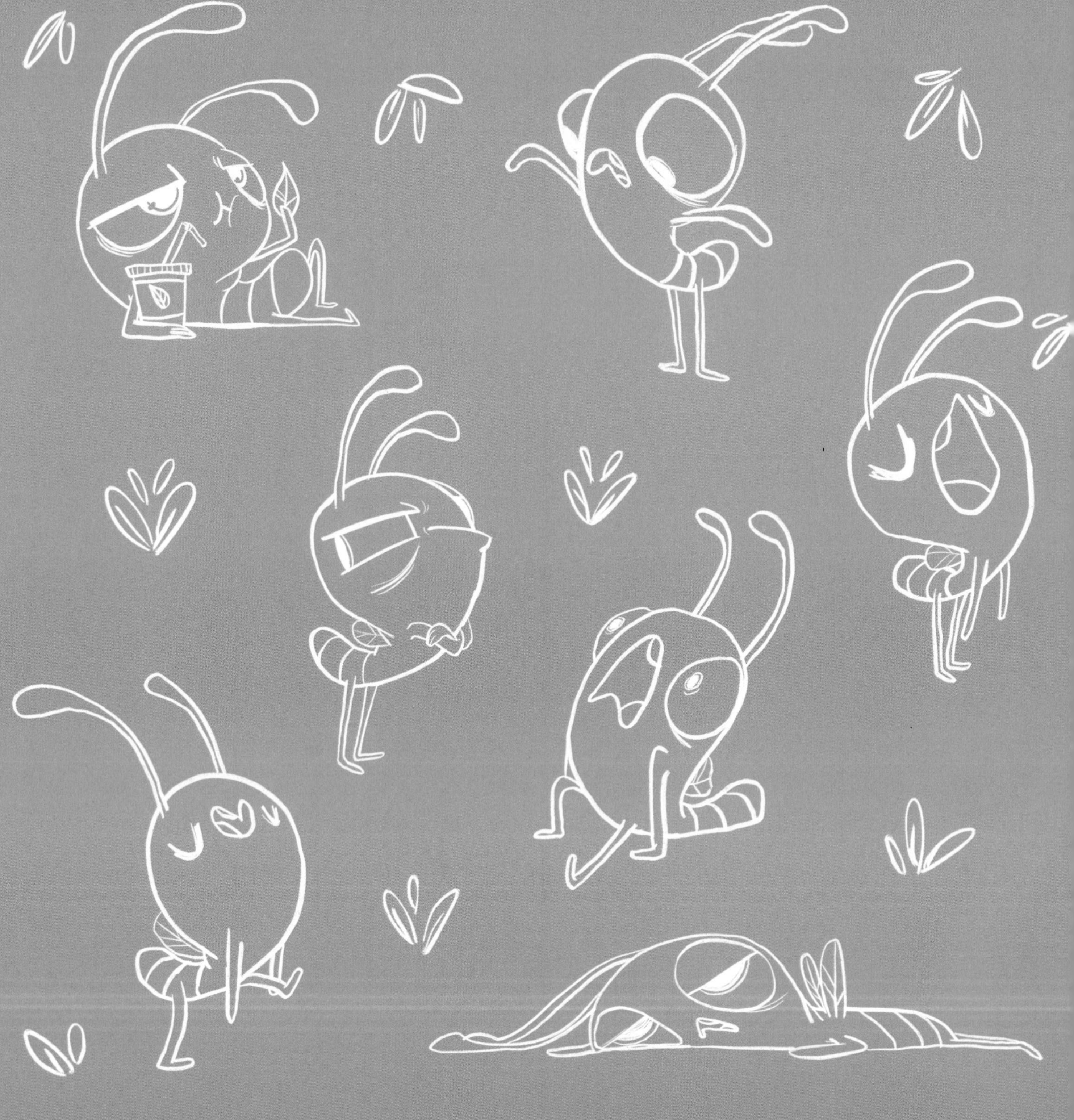

Made in the USA
Middletown, DE
16 December 2020

Do you have a lazy bug in your family?

ISBN 978-1-952821-05-9

Can't Get Me!

Written By
Lisa Lynn MacDonald

Illustrated By
Madison Mastrangelo

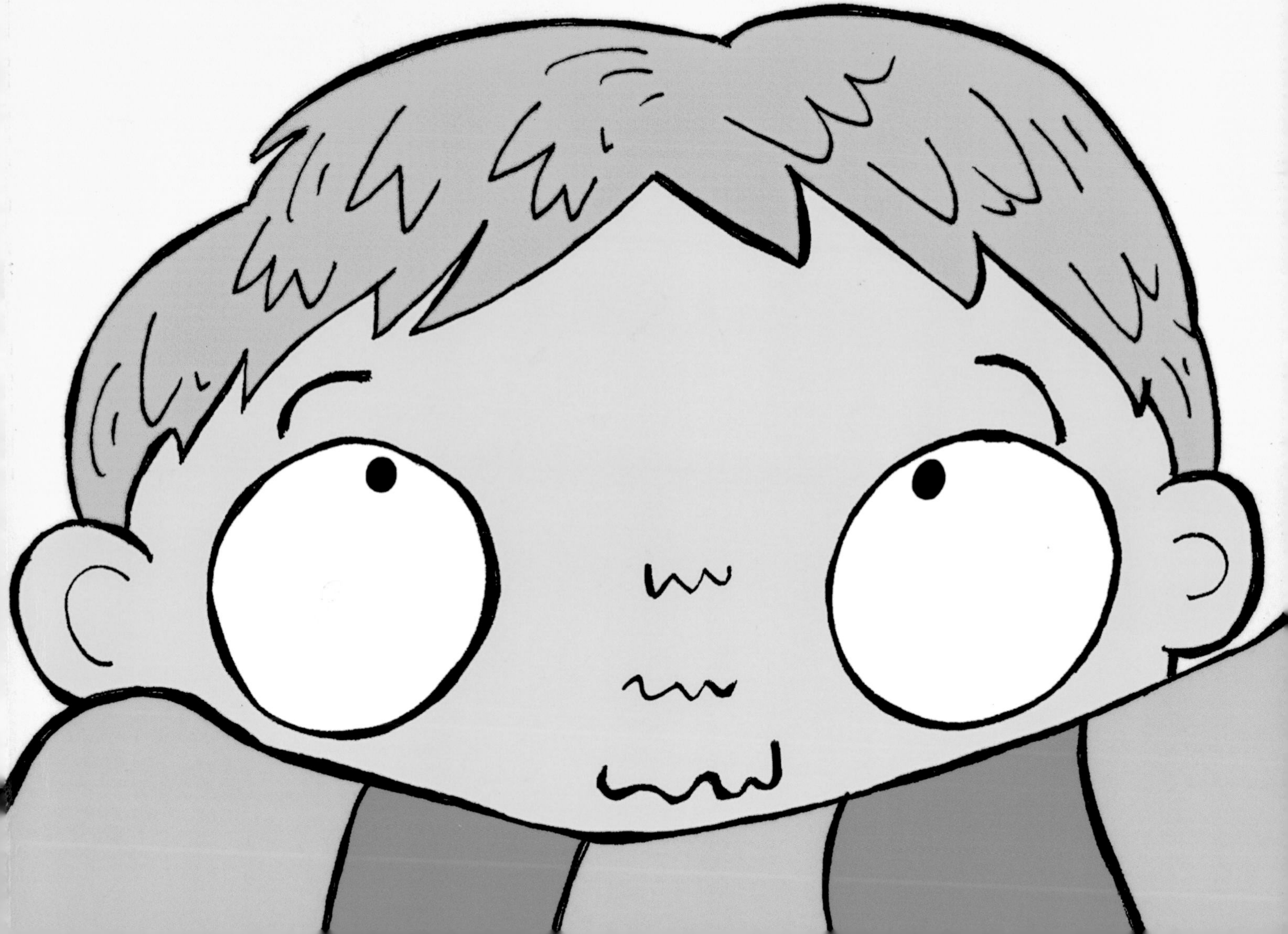